"DANIEL, WILL YOU DO SOMETHING FOR ME?" Samantha asked.

"Sure. What—"

"I've bought a dead bolt lock. Would you mind installing it on the door to my apartment?"

She was afraid? The thought hadn't crossed his mind. Then it hit him. There was already a lock on the main entrance to the house, and he was the only other person with a key.

He took the lock from her and nodded. "I'll do it today."

"Thanks."

"Samantha."

She met his gaze, and for a moment he saw a flash of something he hadn't seen in years. Interest. Desire?

"Is anything wrong?"

"No."

Just "no." No explanation, no reassuring words. Her gaze darted to his hand, and he felt his breath catch as he realized he was caressing the soft skin of her arm. He pulled away as if he'd been burned.

"Are you afraid, Samantha?"

He felt the tension enter her body, though they no longer touched. She met his eyes. "Yes."

He leaned closer. "Are you afraid of me?"

WHAT ARE *LOVESWEPT* ROMANCES?

They are stories of true romance and touching emotion. We believe those two very important ingredients are constants in our highly sensual and very believable stories in the LOVE-SWEPT line. Our goal is to give you, the reader, stories of consistently high quality that may sometimes make you laugh, sometimes make you cry, but are always fresh and creative and contain many delightful surprises within their pages.

Most romance fans read an enormous number of books. Those they truly love, they keep. Others may be traded with friends and soon forgotten. We hope that each LOVESWEPT romance will be a treasure—a "keeper." We will always try to publish

LOVE STORIES YOU'LL NEVER FORGET
BY AUTHORS YOU'LL ALWAYS REMEMBER

The Editors

FLIRTING
WITH FIRE

KRISTEN
ROBINETTE

BANTAM BOOKS
NEW YORK · TORONTO · LONDON · SYDNEY · AUCKLAND

FLIRTING WITH FIRE

A Bantam Book / April 1998

ISBN 0-553-44582-0

Published simultaneously in the United States and Canada

*Bantam Books are published by Bantam Books, a division of Bantam Dou-
bleday Dell Publishing Group, Inc. Its trademark, consisting of the words
"Bantam Books" and the portrayal of a rooster, is Registered in U.S.
Patent and Trademark Office and in other countries. Marca Registrada.
Bantam Books, 1540 Broadway, New York, New York 10036.*

PRINTED IN THE UNITED STATES OF AMERICA

OPM   10 9 8 7 6 5 4 3 2 1

To my grandmother,
"the Divine Ms. Emm,"
who is truly a steel magnolia.

And in loving memory of
Nell Sullivan,
my aunt and my friend.

PROLOGUE

The handwriting sample was easy to analyze. Samantha Delaney traced the indention of the man's signature with a practiced hand. Erratic pressure, forceful, exaggerated first letter of the last name. He was egotistical and likely moody. She made a quick note in the margin of the sample. Definitely not someone Daleco, her largest client, should hire.

The ringing of the telephone cut through the quiet of her apartment, and Samantha jumped, the point of the red pencil crumbling against the unfinished report. "Dammit," she muttered.

And damn DiCarlo for making her afraid of her own shadow.

The ringing was replaced by the mechanical hum of the fax machine, and eventually she heard a single sheet of paper drop into the receiving tray. She threw the useless pencil down and grabbed a pen from her desk drawer, intentionally keeping her back to the machine.

The fax was probably just a request from a client, she lied to herself. She would check it later.

The phone rang again, seconds after the first transmission was completed. Samantha felt a familiar tightening in her shoulders. Maybe something was wrong with the machine, she thought. But she knew better. It was happening again.

Just like the last time.

She hated herself for the fear, the weakness. She hadn't hesitated for a moment when the state's prosecutor had requested that she testify in the murder trial of Dante DiCarlo. Whether DiCarlo's business partner had actually committed suicide or been murdered by DiCarlo was a question for the jury. Whether DiCarlo had forged his partner's signature on legal documents was the question the prosecutor wanted her to answer. The answer was yes.

DiCarlo was now going to great lengths to keep her from testifying to that fact.

Samantha pushed away from her desk, took a deep breath, and stood. Her bare feet sunk into the plush white carpet as she crossed the spacious office to the apartment window. Below her the city of Atlanta stretched like a lazy woman. Lights twinkled in the darkness, winking and sparkling with activity. Resting, but never asleep, she thought.

And somewhere out there was Dante DiCarlo and a small army of people more than willing to do his bidding, anxious to carry out his wishes.

She rubbed chill bumps from her arms, suddenly feeling exposed at the wide expanse of glass. The apartment was more than her workplace—it was her home. But tonight the contemporary chrome-and-glass furnishings, the clean lines of the white carpet and sofa, left her cold. Slowly she turned from the window, her gaze falling on the fax machine.

It was time to face facts. She crossed back to her office, the tension in her shoulders mounting until she felt as if the tendons would snap. Her hand reached for the facsimile, and she watched the motion as though she were dreaming. Finally she lifted the paper. Scrawled across it in broad, bold letters was the word *BOOM*.

"Not again," she whispered.

The fax hummed as the second transmission was received, and another sheet of paper emptied into the tray. She couldn't bear to touch it. But she didn't have to. In plain cursive writing was the word *You're*.

A hysterical laugh escaped her as she examined the telephone number where the second fax had originated. A South Carolina area code. She looked at the first message. Alabama. Last week they had both been from Florida. He was playing games, proving how far his reach extended.

She knew the phone would ring a third time, yet still jumped when it did. She wanted to cry, to rant and scream, but was paralyzed with fear instead. Of course she knew how the last message would read, but stood there, waiting. She had no other choice. It would be the last piece of the puzzle, the last reason she needed to leave Atlanta.

The fax machine sucked up a sheet of paper, then

spit out the last part of DiCarlo's warning. Samantha lifted the paper and read the only word written on the page: *dead.*

The final message had been sent from Tennessee. She didn't have to guess at the meaning.

She was surrounded, trapped.

She laid the papers with their macabre message side by side on her desk. "Boom. You're dead," she whispered as she read them aloud. The words hung in the silence of her office.

It was time to go.

ONE

At first the rain had been welcome, had felt like a cleansing. The refreshing feeling had been a fleeting comfort, though, vanishing as easily as her old life. Samantha gripped the steering wheel and squinted into the darkness. Now the rain fell in continuous sheets, sending a curtain of steam up from the asphalt to further block her vision.

The moist air mixed with the car's heater to form an acrid smell, and an overwhelming sense of dread washed over her. She swallowed hard and fought the urge to cry. She couldn't afford to let down her guard. Not yet.

A bolt of lightning lit the horizon, followed by a crack of thunder that permeated the car's quiet interior. The lines on the country road were faded, and the rainwater reflected the glare of the headlights at every curve, making the simple act of keeping the car on the road a life-or-death situation. Finally, the hazy blue circle of a streetlamp glowed ahead. Samantha breathed a sigh of relief. She'd made it to Scottsdale, Georgia. All she had to do was find the Caldwell place, and this nightmare would end.

Leaning toward the passenger's seat, she reached into the open cavity of her purse, searching for the scrap of paper with the directions to the rental house written on it. Nothing. She gently applied the brakes, slowing as the car approached the first sign of civilization she'd encountered in over an hour—a stop sign. Still, no luck.

Samantha pulled the heavy purse onto her lap, her fingers digging through the contents until she finally felt a small piece of paper. She glanced at it. The directions. When she looked up again he was there.

And she was going to hit him.

Her foot slammed against the brake. The car instantly went into a tailspin and headed broadside toward the intersection. Straight for the hooded figure who crouched before her.

No! The word echoed in her head as she steered into the skid. It was inevitable, yet the solid thump of the car against his body sent a wave of nausea surging against the back of her throat. Finally the car stopped careening, sliding almost gently until her back wheels came to rest in a shallow ditch.

It took a moment before she could pry her foot off the brake and release her seat belt. Samantha looked over her shoulder, her eyes searching the dimly lit road.

She focused on a dark figure. Slowly he moved

against the pavement, then began to crawl to the other side of the road.

"Oh my God," she whispered. She pressed trembling fingers against her mouth. "Thank you. Thank you. He's alive."

By the time she opened the car door and ducked into the rain, the figure had reached the far side of the road. She watched as he slumped against the shoulder, the tall weeds almost hiding him entirely.

Samantha cupped her hands together and shouted, "I'm coming. Are you okay?"

She squinted, peering through the rain. The streetlight barely cast enough light to make out the figure at all. Seconds passed but no answer came. You idiot, she thought. Of course he was hurt. You just hit him with a car.

"Stay where you are. Sit down." She gestured with her hands. "I'm coming."

She shoved the key into the trunk, and the heavy lid lifted with maddening mechanical slowness. Grabbing the small first-aid kit inside, she slammed the trunk closed.

But when she turned back to the road, he was gone.

No. Her eyes were playing tricks on her. She glanced frantically up and down the section of dark road. He was gone. Rainwater dripped into her eyes. She looked down at the first-aid kit, then back toward the road. Help. She needed help.

Dropping the kit, she ran back to the car. She plunged her hand into her purse and retrieved her cell phone. Dear God, why hadn't it been the first thing she thought of? With shaking fingers, she dialed 911, leaned back against the car, and closed her eyes. She had time for a quick prayer before the switchboard operator answered. She shouted the details of the accident into the phone and waited impatiently for the woman to confirm the report in her slow southern drawl.

"Hurry!" She threw the phone into the passenger's seat, then grabbed her umbrella, rationalizing that she'd find the person faster without a torrent of rainwater in her eyes. Tracing her way back to the stop sign, she hesitated. There was no blood, of course. The rain would have washed it away. She tried to judge the distance, to estimate exactly where the person would have crawled to.

She ran to the other side of the road, where she'd last seen him. A shallow ditch separated the road from a thick tangle of underbrush. "Hey! Where are you?" Samantha yelled. She raised her voice even louder. "Come back." She felt the telltale stinging of tears. "I want to help," she called again, though the emotion in her voice choked out her intention to shout.

Headlights zigzagged behind her, and she turned to find that a sheriff's car had pulled up. The big vehicle rocked as it was shifted into park, then the blue emergency lights flashed on, illuminating the dark stretch of road. When the ordinary-looking sheriff emerged, she thought he must be the most welcome sight she'd ever seen.

The burly sheriff snapped a cellophane cover over the broad rim of his hat before placing the hat, with precise arrangement, on his head. The beam from his flashlight blinded her. "You make an emergency call?"

How many other people were racing up and down the side of a dark road in the rain? Of course she'd made the call. Still, the reality of what she was about to say made her want to bolt.

"Yes." She clutched the umbrella until her fingers ached. "I've hit someone."

The flashlight flickered from her eyes and danced across the shoulder of the road. The sheriff made a muffled remark into the receiver of his radio before he walked over to her. "You sure?"

For a moment she considered the idea that she hadn't actually hit someone. But she had. She raised her voice, half to be heard over the rain, half out of indignation. "Of course I'm sure."

"Where are they?"

"He's— I don't know. I went to get my first-aid kit, and he disappeared."

"You mean he just up and vanished?"

"I explained that to the dispatch person," Samantha said through gritted teeth. She felt near hysteria, and the sheriff seemed more ready to question her sanity than to help. "He was wearing a black hooded jacket and dark pants." She pointed toward the road. "He was there, but he must have gone into the woods." Her voice sounded strange, and her head began to buzz. "We've got to find him!"

"Calm down, miss."

The flashlight was in her eyes again, a glowing ball of light and color. She felt the rain soaking through her leather flats and her slacks, chilling the lower half of her legs. Yet her face was hot, glowing hot like the flashlight that blotted out her vision.

"Miss?"

The colors in the beam of light swirled, merging with the flashing blue lights of the sheriff's car. They danced for a moment before spiraling down at nauseating speed.

Then there was black. Unhurried, safe, empty. A welcome nothingness that was just black.

"Miss Delaney?"

The heavy rain had stopped, reduced to a gentle pattering. Samantha was comfortable, more relaxed than she'd been since the death threats had begun. Her fingers stroked a thick blanket, and she pulled the rough fabric to her chin.

"Are you okay?"

The voice penetrated the silence a second time, more commanding. Irritating. She opened her eyes and with some effort focused on her surroundings. The dome light dimly lit the stark, official interior of the sheriff's car, and the fleshy folds of his face were creased into a concerned frown.

Was she okay? Her first instinct was to say yes, to give him the polite answer. That was always the answer everyone wanted to hear, wasn't it? But the truth was, she didn't feel okay. She felt like screaming. No, more like hiding until the storm—and the trial—passed. Until she felt safe again.

She sat upright and smoothed a long tendril of damp hair from her forehead. "What happened?"

"You fainted, Miss Delaney."

She glanced down to see her billfold opened to her driver's license, then looked out the windshield, focusing on the flashing light from the sheriff's car that still lit the darkness outside. Of course, there had been an accident. . . . Reality came back to her then, with crashing sureness.

"Did you find him?" she asked slowly, fearing the answer.

"Yes." The sheriff studied her face for a moment. "But you'll be relieved to know it was just a dog."

"What?" She shoved the blanket from her legs and moved to open the car door. "That's impossible."

His fingers wrapped firmly around her upper arm. "It was a big dog, a black Lab to be exact. It seems he walked to the edge of the woods before he died." He moved his hand to her shoulder and patted her as though she were a child. "Everything's all right now."

The rain drifted through the cracked car door, as if determined to finish soaking her. She shook her head to clear her thoughts. "But it wasn't a dog. I saw—"

"A person in dark pants and a hooded jacket." The sheriff met her eyes. "I imagine with the rain and all, it looked a lot like a person." He shifted his gaze to her open purse, to the prescription bottle that was visible from any angle. "I'd say you were lucky this time."

It took a moment for the meaning of his words to sink in. She started to reach for her purse, then stifled the urge. Her doctor had insisted on writing her a prescription for a mild sedative, one to help her sleep. She had resisted but finally decided to have it filled before leaving the city. Just in case moving to Scottsdale didn't end the nightmare her life had become lately.

And judging from the way it was going, her streak of bad luck was just getting started.

She hesitated until her anger was under control. "If you think I'm on medication—" She stopped, realizing how pathetic that argument was about to sound. "If you think I was driving under the influence of medication—"

He picked up the radio receiver, ignoring her. "Jean, did you ever get Caldwell on the phone?"

The radio cracked with static before a female voice responded. "Still no answer."

Samantha was taken aback. "How did you know?"

The sheriff held up the piece of paper with the directions to the Caldwell house. "Excuse the invasion of your privacy, but I needed to find out who you were, where you were headed." She couldn't miss the skepticism in his expression. "You were out like a light, you know."

"If I fainted, it was due to the accident."

"Oh, you passed out all right." He adjusted his considerable weight in the car's seat, and the imitation leather squeaked against the motion. The pause was as condemning as his words when he spoke again. "Miss Delaney, I'm willing to overlook the circumstances of your accident this time, but—"

"Francis, what the hell do you think you're doing?"

The car door was jerked open, and the void was

filled with blue-jeans clad thighs and a dripping rain slicker. The man leaned down, and the most piercing green eyes she'd ever seen raked her from head to toe.

"Sam Delaney?"

She nodded.

She thought she heard him curse before he turned toward the sheriff. "I don't know what happened here, but you have no right to interrogate anyone without a damned good reason." He looked back at Samantha, his square jaw set in an angry line. "Much less question a woman alone. And in the privacy of your patrol car, I might add."

The sheriff threw back his head and chuckled, but his expression altered slightly. Begrudging respect, Samantha thought.

"I musta missed you going to law school. Last time I checked you didn't make it through that fancy college—"

"Get out of the car."

Samantha thought the words were for the sheriff until she looked up to find the man's gaze locked on her. Part of her resented the bluntly issued command, but the overwhelming urge to get out of the patrol car won. The man barely backed up enough for her to squeeze through the door opening. Almost as an afterthought, she leaned back in to snatch her purse from the sheriff's grip.

She leveled a stare at the big man. "I take it you have all the information you'll need to fill out a report?"

The sheriff ran his tongue over his bottom lip and shook his head. "There's no need for a report, miss."

Samantha felt her pulse pounding against her temples. She wasn't crazy and she wasn't high. And she was in no mood for his condescending tone. "Let me warn you, sheriff." She jabbed her finger in his direction as she spoke. "You won't hear the end of it until I'm certain a report has been filed."

When she straightened, Samantha found herself enveloped in the stranger's rain slicker. Before she could thank him, a firm push to her shoulder told her there wasn't time. The gentle rain had become a deafening downpour again. "Let's go," he shouted.

As she spotted a beat-up old pickup truck parked a few yards away, her nerve faltered. She was headed into the night with a stranger. Not to mention the fact that she'd just told off the local law enforcement. She glanced at her own car, stuck firmly in the ditch, then back to the man. Swallowing hard, she raised her voice. "I have to ask you—"

Thunder rolled in the distance, and she gasped as the cool wind blew a sheet of rain and wet leaves into her face. Without his slicker, the rain was pelting the man, pouring over his thick blond hair and his T-shirt, soaking his jeans.

"Not now," he said, and headed for the truck.

Samantha followed him at a jog and entered the cab of the truck when he opened the passenger door. Once inside, she pulled the wet slicker from her head and shoulders and tossed it onto the gritty floorboard. He entered beside her in a rush of wind and rain before pulling the door closed.

He reached across her to the glove box, which was missing its door, and removed a scrap of worn terry towel. He ran it across his face and over his hair before turning toward her. She couldn't see, couldn't read his expression in the darkness.

"What did you want to ask me?" His voice was smooth and mellow.

Samantha knew that, had there been any light, he would have seen the uncertainty in her eyes. She cleared her throat and resisted the urge to bolt from the truck.

"Who are you?"

TWO

Her dark eyes were as large and innocent as a doe's. And as wary, Daniel thought. The nearby streetlamp cast just enough light for him to make out her features. She didn't look like the Sam Delaney he'd expected. She was female. Beautiful, vulnerable, and distracting as hell. An old anger tightened in his chest. Well, that's what he got for doing business through the mail.

He cranked the engine. "I'm Daniel Caldwell."

For a moment her expression registered relief, but just as quickly turned suspicious. "The sheriff called you?"

"No. I was already on my way." He met her puzzled gaze. "You're only a few blocks from the house. I was outside and saw the emergency lights."

She frowned. "Why would you go to the scene of an accident?"

"We keep an eye on one another around here." A

little too closely sometimes, he thought. He shrugged. "This isn't Atlanta."

She dropped her gaze and shifted in the seat. "Yes, I've noticed. The sheriff was a veritable welcome wagon of hospitality."

Droplets of rain clung to her auburn hair, and a few beads of moisture rested against her cheek. He found himself staring at those stray droplets, fighting the urge to wipe them away. He wouldn't, of course, for more reasons than he could count. Not the least of which was the anxious expression she wore on that ivory-smooth face. She looked ready to jump from the truck at a moment's notice.

"Yeah, well," he said, "some things never change. Francis has been a jerk since the third grade."

She nodded, and he thought he saw a smile play briefly about her lips. "So why were you outside in this weather?"

He looked down at her hands. She folded then refolded them in her lap, twisting and fidgeting with a diamond ring on her right hand. A large diamond ring, he noted before his mind returned to the situation at hand. She was nervous. And hopefully that explained all the questions. The last thing he needed right now was questions—especially those he couldn't answer.

"No good reason," he lied. "So what made you decide to park your car in the ditch?"

She shook her head and looked out the window. "I hit someone." Her voice was so low, he barely heard her. "The sheriff insisted that it was a dog, but—"

"You what?" Daniel felt a cold terror grip him.

"He just appeared out of nowhere. It was so dark and the person was wearing a dark jacket. It all happened so fast . . ."

A dark jacket. Oh my God. Daniel felt as if someone had punched him in the gut. *David . . .*

He gripped the gearshift. "What did he look like?"

"I don't know really." There was a faraway look in her eyes as she gestured with her hands. "The jacket was the kind with a hood."

The worry he'd been fighting over the past couple of hours turned to panic. He should never have let David go walking alone. What had he been thinking? Daniel slammed the truck into first gear. "Was he hurt?"

She grabbed the dashboard for balance as he pulled onto the road. "You believe me?"

"Of course I believe you. You'd have to be an idiot not to know whether or not you hit someone. Now answer the question—was he hurt?"

"No." She snapped her seat belt into place as the truck plowed through a pothole. "At least I don't think so. I don't know how, but he crawled away." She glanced back over her shoulder. "What about my car? My luggage is—"

"I'll come back after it."

Thank God, she didn't object. He glanced at Samantha Delaney's petite silhouette perched on the seat next to him. Her eyes were on the road, her knuckles white against the dashboard as he pushed the old pickup to accelerate. He felt a surge of admiration.

She'd endured a hell of an introduction to Scottsdale that night.

But he couldn't stop to think about that right now.

You'll never be able to care for him by yourself, Daniel.

His mother's words came back to haunt him. Her expression always altered, revealing her distaste when she spoke of his younger brother.

Just be grateful that you weren't cursed. I knew from the moment he was born that he wouldn't be like you. He's not like other people and never will be. . . .

"Hang on," he muttered, as he maneuvered around another pothole.

Out of the corner of his eye he saw her brace her shoulder against the rusted door of the pickup. She seemed capable enough. That was good. Because right now he had all he could handle.

He glanced in her direction and felt a pang of regret. Samantha Delaney was on her own.

"This is it." Daniel practically shouted the words as he clambered from the cab of the pickup and into the rain.

Samantha looked up at the stately white columns of the old house. A large chandelier lit the porch and the sculpted boxwoods that bordered it. She was no expert, but the architecture looked antebellum. She frowned. Not only was the house beautiful, it was huge. There had to be some mistake. There was no way the modest rent listed in Daniel Caldwell's classified ad was for this house. Her stomach dropped. She'd painstakingly planned every detail. The last thing she needed was for her plans—her escape—to fall through.

A blast of cold, damp air stole her thoughts as Daniel flung open her door. "Let's go."

"But I—"

"We can talk about it inside." He threw the slicker around her shoulders, and before she knew it they were jogging across the leaf-scattered lawn toward the house.

"I don't understand." She watched as he produced a key from his jeans pocket and fitted it into the lock. "Is this the rental house?"

He looked over his shoulder to meet her eyes. "Is there a problem?"

Seeing his features clearly for the first time, she temporarily faltered. "N-no. Not at all."

A slight dark stubble covered his square jaw, and, though damp, his dark blond hair fell in straight layers to his shoulders. She would classify his features as somewhere between ruggedly masculine and too-refined to match the long hair and faded blue jeans. But a lady-killer by anyone's standards, she decided. When she met his gaze, she found that the same piercing green eyes she'd encountered earlier were now looking at her with trepidation.

She bit her lip and forced herself to repeat his question in her head. "Nothing's wrong, exactly. It's just more house than I anticipated . . . for the money, I mean."

Daniel didn't answer, just pushed open the door and motioned for her to follow. He flipped on an interior light, illuminating a grand foyer with polished hardwood floors and a graceful staircase. The smell of aged wood and freshly waxed floors welcomed her. Samantha was immediately enveloped in a warmth she hadn't felt for some time. Maybe it was the contrast between the quiet shelter of the house and the storm that raged outside, but she was grateful for the feeling of security.

Then, from the upstairs level, a door slammed. For a moment she felt the old terror return, and the worried frown on her landlord's face didn't help. In the next instant the frown was replaced by the most charming grin she'd ever seen.

"If you're afraid I'm undercharging you, don't worry." He gestured toward the staircase. "The second level is still being renovated, loose shutters and all."

"Oh." For the first time, she noticed that the foyer's Sheetrock was dotted with spackling, and that the wooden planks of the stairs had been stripped of their varnish.

Daniel looked away and nodded. "Your apartment is in the east wing." He cleared his throat. "The west wing has been closed off for some time, and I'm still working on the attic and second story."

Samantha found herself wishing he would turn toward her again so that she could better see his face. But what did that matter? The fact was, it shouldn't. He was a handsome man, athletically built, his demeanor rugged but his eyes kind. She was simply curious.

But the heat that rushed through her body as he looped his arm around her shoulders was sparked by more than curiosity. For a moment she was confused, couldn't imagine why he was touching her.

"I need to check on something." He ushered her, more than a little brusquely, through the interior door that led to her quarters. "Make yourself at home. I'll be back."

She stared after him as he left, until the dull thud of the heavy front door echoed through the big old house. Alone. But safe, she reminded herself. Wasn't that why she was there? Then suddenly, surrounded by the unnatural quiet of the old mansion, she realized it hadn't been the house that made her feel safe.

It had been Daniel Caldwell.

"David!" Daniel flung open the door to the caretaker's cottage. No lights were on, but that wasn't unusual. For a minute all he could hear was his own labored breathing. Then he heard the slow, unmistakable sound of a zipper.

"What on earth?" he whispered. He made his way to a nearby table lamp and switched it on.

As the gentle light illuminated the room, Daniel saw him. David was curled into a corner of the small living room, his battered backpack clutched to his chest. He shielded his eyes from the light with one hand, the hood of his jacket still drawn over his head.

Daniel made a quick assessment of his brother. No blood, no visible injury. He dropped to his knees. "Are you okay?"

David shook his head and tried to unzip his

backpack. The imprint of Samantha's tire marked the olive green canvas, and the outside flap had been ripped away.

Understanding dawned on Daniel, and his stomach knotted.

Intelligent green eyes, identical to his own, looked up at him. "I'm gonna need a new backpack."

Laughter. God, how long had it been since he'd wanted to laugh? It trickled from him at first, then poured out in torrents of relief. Finally Daniel wiped his eyes and hugged his brother to him. David returned the hug, no longer rigid and cold as he'd been just three weeks earlier. Daniel released him and pulled the hood from his brother's head, revealing thick brown curly hair.

He nodded. "I'll get you another backpack."

Where on earth was he? Samantha glanced at her watch. She was tired—no, exhausted. At first she'd sat, like a guest, on the living room sofa. Finally, she'd kicked off her rain-soaked flats, then pulled a cotton throw from the back of the sofa and wrapped it around her shoulders. In the absence of a dry change of clothes, it was the best she could do.

After an hour had passed, she decided to explore her portion of the house. Despite the less-than-perfect start to the night, she had to admit that the apartment was great. As promised, there was a study she could use as her office, a small living room and kitchen, and a large, nicely decorated bedroom. Tomorrow she would ask for a dead bolt lock. Then she'd have everything she needed.

She jumped as the front door rattled.

"Samantha?"

Chill bumps ran the length of her arms. Not because she didn't recognize the voice, but because she wasn't accustomed to hearing her name called so. . . . What exactly *was* different about the way Daniel Caldwell said her name? It sounded so smooth and—unintentionally, she was certain—sensual.

She ran her business solo, out of her home. The men she dealt with were business associates and, more often than not, merely voices over the phone. She'd dated often when she was in her early twenties, yet it had always felt more obligatory than pleasurable—something she was supposed to do. She'd waited to fall in love, waited for the emotion to kick in. It hadn't. Now, a little closer to thirty and a little wiser, the less necessary love and an accompanying man seemed.

Maybe it was because she'd learned that intimacy wouldn't—couldn't—last beyond one night. One of the first rules to surviving in the business world was to know your weaknesses. Samantha knew hers, and the list included a few personal ones she'd never dealt with.

"I'm here," she answered.

He emerged from the shadows of the foyer, now thoroughly soaked by the rain and still totally disarming.

"Is something wrong?" He set her luggage on the carpeted living room floor.

She smiled, a weak attempt to cover her embarrassment as she realized she'd been staring. "No. It's just that I was about to offer you something to dry off with, when I realized I don't know where anything is."

"I'm fine, thanks." He smoothed his damp hair from his eyes. "But the linen closet is next to the bathroom if you need anything."

She crossed the room to take her bags. "Was everything okay—with the car, I mean? I worried when you didn't come right back."

He picked up her bags and headed toward the bedroom without asking. "Everything was fine. I'll get your car in the morning."

She followed him into the dark bedroom, the filtered glow from the streetlamp the only light that entered through the heavy lace curtains. After setting down the luggage, he turned toward her, his expression unreadable in the gloom.

She started toward the bedside lamp, then hesitated. He seemed so at ease in the darkness that the idea of scurrying for the security of a light seemed ridiculous. Cowardly. There were things to fear in her life, and she'd encountered them all in the last few weeks: DiCarlo, death threats, rain-slick roads.

Daniel walked to the window and peered outside. His upper body was outlined by the faint glow of the streetlight that permeated the storm. The damp T-shirt he wore revealed every muscle and curve of his chest, and the room was not only filled with his presence, but his scent. He smelled of fresh rainwater and warm skin, and she felt almost intoxicated by his nearness. But as he let the curtain drop back into place and turned toward her, she realized what was so fascinating about him. It was his eyes. His body might speak of raw strength, but his eyes were gentle.

Yes, she had things to fear. Daniel Caldwell was not one of them.

"I'm staying in the guest cottage out back." He gestured out the window, then walked back out of the room as quickly as he'd entered. "There's no phone yet, but if you need me, you know where to find me."

"Yes, thanks." The truth was, she hadn't even noticed a guest cottage, but relief surged through her at the knowledge that he would be nearby.

He paused, drumming his fingers against the bedroom doorframe for a moment. "Good night," he said finally.

"Good night." She heard his footsteps despite the thick carpeting that covered the hallway floor. "Thank you," she called after him, but doubted he heard.

The front door closed and she was alone again. She sat down on the edge of the bed, the thick old feather mattress inviting her to lie down. But she wouldn't be able to sleep. Not yet. Finally she gave in to the need for light and switched on the bedside lamp. Warm amber light flowed from beneath the globe, illuminating the white matelassé bedspread and rich tones of the cherry bedroom suite that dominated the room.

The furnishings were welcoming, though unfamiliar. She sighed. She would get used to the house eventually. After all, it was a place of refuge, not home.

She unzipped her overnight bag and retrieved a cotton T-shirt, a comfortable pair of sweatpants, and a spiral-bound notebook that contained notes on a work project she hoped to complete. As she hugged the soft, thick sweatpants to her chest, her thoughts flickered over the events of the evening and settled, against her will, on Daniel Caldwell. What was it about him—a total stranger—that had caused her to react so strongly?

She recalled the look of intimidation on the burly sheriff's face when Daniel had flung open the car door. She smiled, remembering the sense of defiance she'd felt as she stepped out of the patrol car and into the storm. Give yourself a break, she thought. He rescued you. How often does that happen?

She slipped into the dry change of clothes and settled the notebook in her lap, but after thirty minutes of trying to concentrate on work, she tossed the paperwork aside in frustration. She looked at her watch. It was well past midnight, and she wasn't the least bit sleepy.

The sedatives were still in her purse, but she had no desire to take one, especially after the sheriff's insinuations. She'd never been comfortable using medicine, and being in strange surroundings made her even less enthusiastic. A glass of water, on the other hand, sounded inviting.

Samantha crawled off the thick mattress and made her way to the bathroom. The fixtures were old but well cared for, and Daniel had seen to it that she had everything she needed. She smiled as she noticed a plastic cup dispenser that held miniature orange-and-yellow paper cups. Definitely not the decorative touch a woman might have chosen, but she appreciated it all the same.

She filled the cup with water and padded back down the hall to her bedroom. Perhaps it was the new surroundings, but she couldn't bring herself to change into a nightgown. The sweatpants and T-shirt were comfortable enough to sleep in, and the thought of wearing a gown made her feel vulnerable. In fact, the idea of even undressing again made her suddenly nervous. She set the paper cup on the nightstand and crossed to the window.

A flash of light in the courtyard between the mansion and the guest cottage caught her eye. A flashlight? Several massive oak trees dotted the lawn, casting dancing shadows as they swayed in the stormy night. Samantha breathed a sigh of relief as she caught a glimpse of a dark figure on the cottage porch.

Daniel.

But then the light flashed a second time from the lawn. She allowed the lace curtain to fall back into place, but continued to watch through it. Then she saw him. Daniel's stride was long and easy, though he walked through the pouring rain. Despite the shadows, his T-shirt was illuminated by the pale blue glow of the streetlamp, and his tall, sinewy build was unmistakable. She ducked as he cast the flashlight beam toward the house for a moment before returning it to the path he took through the courtyard.

Her gaze darted back to the guest cottage. If she hadn't seen Daniel on the porch, then who? An image of the sheriff's skeptical expression returned to remind her of another shadowy figure she'd seen that night.

Or one she'd thought she'd seen.

Turning her head, she stared at the phone on the bedside table. She recalled steady green eyes and broad shoulders, recalled her feeling of relief when Daniel had literally put himself between her and the sheriff. It was a good thing the guest house didn't have a phone, because more than anything in the world, she wanted Daniel Caldwell to come back.

THREE

Daniel clasped Leonard Moses on the shoulder. "I appreciate you coming by to keep an eye on David."

"Glad to help out." Moses cleared his throat and smoothed a thin strand of silver hair from his forehead. "The antique shop never sees much business on Mondays, anyway."

Moses had barely aged a day in all the years Daniel had known him, but that morning the creases around his eyes and mouth were deep, betraying his seventy-odd years. Daniel knew him too well to be fooled. It was obvious that Moses didn't approve of his decision to bring David home.

Get used to it, he told himself. Moses's reaction would be mild in comparison to what the good citizens of Scottsdale would treat him to once they found out about David. There would be more questions than answers then. In fact, there would be hell to pay.

It was a rare occasion when he allowed himself to

think that far ahead. He'd operated on a day-to-day basis for so long that planning anything was foreign to him. The day was coming, though, when David could no longer hide from the probing eyes of the town. A stab of guilt hit him. He'd told himself that his brother needed time to adjust before letting others know. But was it that or was it a back door—his own form of security—if he failed?

He thought he'd stopped caring long ago what others thought. He'd learned at an early age that reputation was merely opinion, often wrong but always final. He'd also learned that there was no such thing as a menial job, no pride that couldn't be overcome. Not if you wanted to survive.

This time, however, it wasn't just him. And he wouldn't simply be telling the people of Scottsdale that David was back. He would be telling them that his brother was still alive. As though he'd seen it only yesterday, he could easily picture David's obituary alongside his father's in the local newspaper.

A few members of the community had sincerely grieved for his father and his brother. Most, however, had treated his father's death with the same pseudosincerity that Daniel Caldwell, Senior, had extended to them over the years. Small-town politician to the end, his father had drifted through life as if it were an endless row of handshakes—more concerned with appearances than friends, finding more affection for alcohol than family.

And David? He'd been treated as merely an oddity.

A tragic life, a tragic death. Daniel felt his jaw muscles ache and realized he was clenching his teeth.

"Thanks," he said to Moses. He retrieved his tool belt from the floor, strapping it over his hips. "One more downpour like we had last night and that roof might not hold."

Moses nodded, looking as if he wanted to say something, but didn't. Instead, he picked up the hammer from the floor and handed it to Daniel. "Is everything okay? With David, I mean."

He met his friend's concerned gaze. "Yeah. David's sleeping. His doctor said to expect that. Nothing's changed. His days and nights have been reversed for years."

Moses ran his hand over his jaw. "What do you do at night?"

Daniel laughed. "It's more like what I *don't* do. Sleep." The worried frown on his friend's face deepened, and Daniel held up his hand. "I'm managing. Really. David was just unusually restless last night."

He intentionally avoided telling Moses about Samantha and the accident. After all, David hadn't actually been hurt, only emotionally rattled. Besides, he wanted to keep that failure to himself. Lord knows he'd had enough public ones.

Moses broke the eye contact to examine his boots. "Look, son, no one admires you more than I do for wanting to bring the boy home, but—"

"He's hardly a boy anymore."

Moses paused, then tapped his temple with his fingertips. "He is in here, son."

"I'm not convinced of that." Daniel shoved the hammer into the leather loop of the tool belt. "We've been through this."

He watched frustration settle about the older man's features as Moses turned to look out the window. The only view from the guest cottage was the looming, aging mansion. A constant reminder of days—of a life—now passed. He could almost follow Moses's train of thought. The damage was no longer visible, but the scars remained. On the interior of the old house and inside them all.

"I've wanted to bring David home for the last thirteen years, but I couldn't. Not as long as Mother was his legal guardian."

Moses turned to face him, his expression a mixture of resignation and pain.

"She might not have left me much else when she died," Daniel continued, "but she left me David. This is his home, too, and he has every right to be here."

"You're right. I just watched you and your mother suffer through so much . . ." A gray pallor washed over Moses's face. "I never made any secret that I would have gladly taken your daddy's place. I loved your mother. She deserved better." Moses shook his head. "She shouldn't have stayed with your father all those years."

"You're right about that."

Moses nodded. "About David . . . I just worry. What will happen when folks find out he's still alive? Have you actually thought that through?"

"There's no need to worry." Even as he spoke the

words, he knew it wasn't true. Daniel worked to control the old pain that threatened to rise to the surface. "I can take care of David and I can handle any grief this town wants to dish out. If you can't stay—"

"No, no. I can stay."

The hurt look on his friend's face brought instant regret. Moses was the only one who would bother to worry about him. Hell, he'd been the only one to bother for the past thirteen years. There was a time when the Caldwell name had commanded instant attention, instant concern. But respect had been replaced by curiosity and pity so long ago, he hardly recalled anything else. One minute he'd been a carefree young man, a child of privilege, the mayor's son—

"Just don't forget"—Moses cast a second look out the window and lowered his voice to a whisper—"Just don't forget the reason David was sent away in the first place."

Daniel suddenly felt cold, as if the chill fall air had permeated the room when he wasn't paying attention. *He has to be put away. Just look what he's done to us, to your father*. His mother's words emerged from the past to taunt him, still angry and still accusing.

In his mind's eye he could still see David as he'd been. Different? Yes. But they'd shared the secret world of brothers. In the dark of night David would sit, still as a statue, while Daniel read to him from *Robinson Crusoe*, a flashlight illuminating the pages of the book. Together they would sneak from the house on moonlit nights, walking for hours through the woods, down the secret paths and country roads that only children know.

Did shadows exist at night? Daniel knew they did. Because David had been his shadow.

"Daniel?"

"He was just a boy." Daniel ran his hand through his hair to mask the emotion that coursed through him. "An eight-year-old boy playing with matches."

"Yes, and eight-year-old boys accidentally start fires. Happens every day." Moses paused until Daniel met his gaze. "But you and I both know that David wasn't—isn't—like other boys. For God's sake, Daniel, any other eight-year-old boy would have been asleep in his bed at three o'clock in the morning."

"That's enough."

Moses looked away and sighed. "Lord knows you've seen enough hardship. You have every right to want the only family you have left near you, but maybe it's tempting fate to bring David home."

Tempting fate. He thought back on the last thirteen years. Something in his mother had snapped the night of the fire. As the charred remains of her home crumbled around her, she'd entered a fantasy world where wealth and status still existed. Daniel, on the other hand, had had a crash course in reality. For a minute the weariness crept back. He felt the grief for a lost youth, the physical exhaustion of rebuilding as best he could, providing for his mother . . . burying his father.

Then the cynical determination that had carried him through kicked in. Tempting fate? No. By God, he'd been in charge since he was barely twenty years old, and nothing was about to stop him now.

His mother had finally found peace. His brother had come home. An image of Samantha Delaney—of warm brown eyes and auburn hair—flashed in his mind.

No, nothing could get in his way now. His own life had just begun.

Samantha printed out the document. The few simple lines represented another step toward taking charge of her life. She snapped her notebook computer shut and dialed the telephone number of the local newspaper. Within a few minutes, the classified ad for a secretary had been placed. Now she only needed someone competent but friendly, communicative but quiet enough to work side by side in a small area. A nonsmoker. Punctual. She smiled. That should be a breeze in a town the size of Scottsdale.

She stood and crossed the small office to the kitchen. Autumn sunlight bathed the cheerful little room in a warm glow. In the light of day she could make out the unevenness of the floor and more than a few large cracks in the plaster that betrayed the age of the otherwise graceful house.

Her first instinct upon waking had been to find Daniel Caldwell, but she'd resisted. Instead she'd taken time to explore the apartment, familiarizing herself with every creak of the floors, every nook and closet. Every hiding place, she admitted. She turned the sink tap to hot and filled a daisy-patterned mug she'd found in the pantry. Dropping in a tea bag—one of the few "necessary" items she'd packed—she watched the familiar swirl of orange streak the water.

Daniel struck her as someone who would be in touch when it was necessary, and out of sight when it wasn't. She felt an irrational niggling of disappointment. But hadn't she come there to be alone, to find much-needed distance from her old life? She shook her head. Fear. It made rational people do—need—crazy things.

Without warning, the image of a dark-cloaked person flashed in her head. She closed her eyes and leaned against the counter. Could it have been only a dog she'd hit? If she could just believe that. In either case, she was powerless to do anything about it. Well, almost.

She retrieved a notepad and pencil from her office and returned to the kitchen. Organize. That was what she always did when things tried to get out of hand. She paused, thinking. When was the last time her life had threatened to get out of control? Until DiCarlo entered the picture, she could hardly recall any time. At least not since her parents' deaths. She instinctively reached for her mother's diamond wedding ring and positioned it exactly on her finger.

Things got out of control only when you let them, she reminded herself as she scribbled the words *To Do*, across the top of the blank sheet of paper. First on the list was a visit to the sheriff's office, though she doubted it would do her much good. Then she would check with the local doctor and the closest hospital.

After all, if she'd actually hit someone—and she had—wouldn't they seek help?

Samantha stuck the mug into a microwave she'd discovered in a corner of the kitchen and turned the dial to the minute button. The microwave was old and small, and she couldn't help but wonder if Daniel had gone out of his way to provide it, just as he'd seen to her other needs beforehand. She looked around as she waited for the tea to heat. The house was an odd mix of expensive furnishings, such as the antique cherry bedroom suite and fine linens, and make-do comforts, such as the cheap paper cup dispenser and decrepit microwave.

The sound of an electric saw tore through the quiet house, the shrill noise vibrating across the hardwood floors of the foyer and echoing against the high plaster ceilings of the kitchen. She retrieved the tea from the microwave, dropped the soggy tea bag into the sink, and followed the screeching.

The smell of freshly cut lumber hit her as she opened the interior door that separated her quarters from the rest of the house. The saw was being used upstairs, and she climbed the staircase to the second story. The house must have been huge before it was sectioned off for the apartment, she realized. But now the second story was empty, as far as she could see. She paused on the landing to look down the long hall that connected the east and west wings. Scuffed hardwood flooring covered its length, brightened now and again by patches of sunlight that marked the open doors to various rooms.

The noise was still above her, and as she continued up the second flight of stairs, the shrill buzzing of the saw stopped. Her footsteps echoed in the quiet emptiness, making her feel like an intruder. She considered turning back but reasoned that she might as well continue since she'd come this far. Besides, she planned to live in the house for the next few months. Wasn't it her right to become familiar with it?

Not to mention that her own safety might depend on it, she added mentally. She took a quick sip of tea and tried to rid herself of the image of Dante DiCarlo that flashed in her head. She'd never laid eyes on the man in person, but it seemed every newspaper photo of him she'd ever seen had managed to capture what she already knew from his handwriting samples. Evil.

The stairwell ended abruptly at the third story, and Samantha found herself facing a closed door. She gently pushed against it with her free hand, and it swung open to reveal a finished attic. Daniel was leaning across a two-by-four, a tape measure in one hand and a pencil in the other.

She propped a shoulder against the doorframe and waited until he'd completed the measurements. "Good morning."

He looked up, his expression telling her that she'd startled him. A boyish, one-sided grin lit his face. "Good morning. Did I wake you?"

She glanced at her watch. It was ten o'clock. Normally she would have been working for hours. That morning, though, she'd been surprised to find that she'd slept well beyond sunup.

"No, not at all. I've just been getting acquainted with the apartment."

He made a quick pencil mark on the lumber before straightening and brushing sawdust from his jeans. "Do you have everything you need?"

Samantha watched the sawdust particles dance in the sunlight slanting in through the gaps in the boarded attic window. Why did she have the sudden urge to say no? She'd always been the strong one, the one who carried on after her parents' deaths, the one who, at the tender age of eighteen, had been called mature beyond her years. And now, when a relative stranger stood before her, asking her a polite but casual question, she wanted to fling herself into his arms and cry on his shoulder.

"Yes, thanks," she answered. "The apartment is great." She took another sip of tea to loosen the lump that had formed in her throat. "I appreciate everything you did for me last night."

He nodded in response, then fished her car keys from his pocket and tossed them to her. "Your car is outside. I didn't see any damage."

"Thank you. You've done too much."

She noticed the muscles in his jaw working before he turned to retrieve the length of wood from the floor. He almost looked embarrassed . . . or angry, she thought.

"Listen," he said, "I wouldn't worry too much about last night. Francis may be an SOB, but he was probably right. It was probably just a dog."

She bit her lip and forced herself not to argue. After

all, he was only attempting to reassure her. "Maybe so. I thought I might drop by the sheriff's office, though, just to check. Can you give me directions?"

He balanced the two-by-four on two battered saw-horses and picked up an electric handsaw before answering. "I doubt that's necessary. I'm sure they would contact you if anything—"

"I really think I should check." Samantha heard the irritation in her voice and immediately regretted letting her guard down. The truth was, *she* was embarrassed. But why? She didn't need his advice, no matter how well-intentioned, and she didn't have time for such childish emotions as embarrassment.

Not only could she stand on her own two feet, she would. She had to. She always had.

Daniel met her gaze, his cool green eyes reflecting intense but unreadable emotion. "Main Street." He flipped on the handsaw, its shrill hum an instant dismissal.

An odd feeling crept through her, unsettling and almost unrecognizable. Then she felt her skin crawl as she recognized it. Her feelings were hurt. She almost dropped the cup of tea. Good God, how long had it been since she felt that emotion?

She stayed long enough to watch the blade cut through the lumber, the broad gap replacing the pencil mark until the board was almost severed. Then she turned and walked away, the sawed wood clamoring against the attic floor just as she pulled the door closed behind her.

So it was play it his way or not at all. But what

possible objection could he have to her double-checking with the sheriff's office? He was her landlord, not her keeper. She descended the stairs and entered her apartment, closing the door with a little more force than necessary. Then she shook her head and laughed. Well, at least she no longer had the urge to fling herself into his arms.

In fact, she felt nothing.

Samantha walked to the kitchen and placed the daisy-embossed mug into the old white sink. Her mother's wedding ring caught the morning sunlight as if demanding her attention, and she stared at the diamond. She could no longer recall the details of her parents' faces, those images long ago replaced by the frozen smiles and poses of photos that remained. But the memories were all too real. At least when she allowed them to slip in. The warmth of her mother's hands, the strength and security in her father's embrace. Love, contentment.

Loss.

Emptiness was safer. She gazed out the window, absently watching a fresh batch of leaves trickle to the ground and dance across the courtyard, caught in a gust of wind.

It was simple, really. Fear bred emotion, and emotion eventually gave way to illogical behavior. She closed her eyes and rid herself of any lingering emotion, summoning the familiar emptiness until all else faded. Then she opened her eyes and straightened her shoulders.

Everything was as it should be again. Safe. Predictable. Empty.

Daniel squinted at the lines of the tape measure, realizing for the first time that there were more shadows in the attic than daylight. Footsteps shuffled on the stairs behind him.

Samantha. What could he say to her now? He'd come off like a jerk that morning, but the last thing he wanted was for her to get Francis poking around town, poking around in his life. Still, he'd caught a glimpse of her face before she disappeared. Her soft brown eyes had looked cold, glassy, and her lips had been set in an angry line. No doubt about it, he'd been a jerk.

"Are we gonna paint tonight?"

For a minute Daniel couldn't breathe. Chill bumps ran the length of his arms as he heard another voice, a child's voice, call to him from the past.

Are we gonna paint tonight?

How many times had he heard that soft voice in the night? How many times had he and his brother escaped into the canvas together, leaving the drunken, angry voices of their mother and father below?

Daniel turned with an easy motion to face David. His brother's face was expressionless, but his luminescent green eyes were clear and expectant.

"Not tonight, Buddy," Daniel answered.

He returned the tape measure to his tool belt. David apparently didn't see the disheveled attic as it was, didn't see that sawdust and lumber—as well as years of neglect—had replaced the canvas and the oils. He felt a pang of longing that hadn't touched him in over a decade. It had been so long since he held a brush in his hand, felt the satisfaction of covering coarse canvas with the smooth beauty of paint.

Instead he'd painted houses. He'd welcomed the jobs, but resented the curious stares as he worked. Most of all he'd shunned the pity.

"Why not?"

Why not? The simple question was as close to an argument, an objection, as David ever presented. He'd uttered those same simple words thirteen years ago.

Just because, he'd answered. Because he'd had someone else on his mind instead of his little brother. Because he'd wanted to escape, to be in the arms of a girl, to bury his hidden pain in the soft folds of her welcoming body.

That decision had cost him. While he'd waited for a rendezvous that never happened, his home—his world—had gone up in flames.

"I've lost my paints." Daniel shrugged and answered his brother as honestly as he could this time. "I don't know where they are."

David nodded.

How could David remember the attic after all these years? he wondered. Was it possible he still recalled the nights he'd tagged along while Daniel painted? He'd been only eight years old. It seemed a lifetime ago to Daniel. He glanced nervously at the boarded window. Maybe the real question wasn't how David remembered, but where Moses was. He walked slowly to the window and looked through the unevenly nailed slats. From his vantage point he could see the guest cottage. Everything was quiet.

Maybe too quiet. A ripple of fear ran through him, a betrayal to his brother's innocence, but there all the same.

Daniel held his hand out to David, refusing to allow his fear get ahead of reason. "Let's go home and I'll look for the paints."

The expression on his brother's face made him want to laugh and cry at the same time. Yes, David had become more physically affectionate over the last few weeks, but the embarrassed look on his face told Daniel one thing: David was too old to hold hands with his big brother.

Daniel felt a fresh surge of hope—or was it simply his own stubbornness? Something had walled his brother away from the world, but there was nothing *wrong* with him. At least not in the way everyone else was determined to believe.

For now, though, he was faced with another problem: How to get David back to the guest cottage without running into Samantha. It wasn't a good idea for David to learn that a stranger was living in the house he had once known as home. Daniel tried to imagine explaining David's past to Samantha without scaring the life out of her. Not good either.

There were two entrances to that part of the attic— through the foyer staircase and through the west wing. Though the west wing's damage was almost completely repaired, the memories remained. At least for him. And since there was no judging what David might remember, he couldn't ask his brother to enter that wing of the house.

Daniel felt the old anger return. The house should have been sold years ago, but his mother had refused. The west wing had been badly damaged by the fire, and once he'd buried his father and started budgeting for David's care, not much of the insurance settlement had been left for repairs. Only the promise of renting the apartment to Samantha had given him the financial reserve to go ahead with the work.

But as desperately as he needed Samantha as a boarder, he wouldn't walk his brother through the west wing.

He clasped David around the shoulders and headed for the door. He could only hope that Samantha was still out. He grinned, recalling her determination to find Francis. Maybe the sheriff had received the brunt of the anger he'd seen shimmering in her eyes. Now that would be sweet.

To his relief, they passed through the foyer and crossed the courtyard without encountering anyone. When they reached the guest cottage, a breathless Moses flung open the door.

"Thank God!"

Daniel pushed David through and closed the door behind them. "What happened?"

Moses shook his head. "I don't know. The only time I wasn't watching him was when I went to the kitchen to get a soda. Next time I checked his room he was gone."

Daniel turned to David. "You shouldn't have left the house." The words were angrier than he intended, and he lowered his voice before he continued. "You remember Moses, don't you? If you needed anything, you should have asked him."

His brother's gaze was fixed out the window, and it was obvious he wasn't listening.

"David?"

David pointed out the window. "She's pretty."

Daniel followed David's stare. It was almost completely dark now, but the porch light spotlighted Samantha as she emerged from her car. The warm glow of the incandescent light accentuated the red of her hair, illuminated her perfect features.

Daniel muttered a curse. He hadn't wanted his brother to know about Samantha. At least not yet. He watched as she balanced a grocery sack against her slender hip and fumbled with the keys. A gust of wind lifted her long hair from her face before she walked up the stairs and disappeared around the corner of the porch.

He wouldn't have argued with his brother, not even if David were capable of understanding, but Samantha Delaney wasn't pretty.

She was beautiful.

FOUR

Samantha set the last of the boxes on the floor of the office. She'd been pleasantly surprised that the delivery truck not only found the Caldwell place that morning, but arrived a day early, even if she had been forced to answer the door in sweatpants and her oldest T-shirt. She wiped her grit-covered hands against her thighs and sighed. Now if the boxes of research notes and reference books were only sorted and put away.

The phone rang, the unfamiliar sound of the bell startling her. She automatically reached for it, but memories of DiCarlo's threats made her hesitate. From outside she heard the delivery truck's heavy diesel engine throb.

The phone rang a second time.

Panic ran through her as the air brakes of the delivery truck hissed like a final warning. The most important piece of her life—her work—had arrived, making the move feel all too permanent. Outside, the delivery truck pulled away, the sound of the engine fading as it left. She was there now, and if DiCarlo had found her, she was finally trapped.

She snatched the phone from its cradle before she lost her nerve. "Hello."

"Samantha Delaney?" a woman's voice, soft and southern, responded.

Relief poured through her, and she sank into her office chair. "Yes."

"My name is Emma Weathers. Douglas Thomas is my uncle."

Samantha frowned. She knew the name but couldn't make the connection.

"Douglas owns the local newspaper. You placed an ad yesterday."

"Yes." She rubbed her forehead, her fingers trembling. "I'm sorry. For a moment I couldn't place the name."

"I hope you don't mind my calling before the ad was even printed, but my uncle knew I was looking for work now that the kids are back in school."

"No. I don't mind at all. In fact, I've been worried that I wouldn't get any response." She smiled, feeling herself relax. She liked Emma's friendly, straightforward way of putting things. "I have to be honest with you, though. This job pushes the definition of *part-time* to the extreme. The hours are few and the pay is even worse."

"Uncle Douglas says you're staying at the Caldwell place?"

"Yes, I'm renting an apartment from Daniel Caldwell." Emma Weathers didn't seem concerned about the salary or the hours. Samantha was surprised but relieved. One of her personality flaws was brutal honesty, and the last thing she needed to do was discourage someone who might be her only potential employee.

"Well . . ." Emma hesitated. "I don't want to seem pushy, but would it be okay if I drop my résumé off this morning?"

Samantha looked down at her dust-covered sweatpants and ran her hand over her loose hair. "You're welcome to drop by if you'll overlook my appearance." She glanced at the piles of books and battered manuscript binders. "Not to mention the appearance of my office. I'm just getting settled in."

"I have two kids and three dogs. Nothing scares me anymore."

A sense of humor. Samantha smiled. If Emma Weathers could type her own name correctly, she was probably going to get the job. "Well, in that case, what time did you have in mind?"

"I was about to run some errands. How does ten-thirty sound to you?"

She glanced at her watch. It was almost ten o'clock and she had too much work to do to stop and get cleaned up. Oh well, Emma might as well get a dose of the real thing. "That's fine. I'll keep an eye out for you."

Samantha placed the receiver back into its cradle. The ringing of the telephone had caused her to break out in a cold sweat. She ran her hand through her hair again, reminding herself that the call had been innocent, willing her hands to stop trembling.

It wasn't beyond reason that DiCarlo could find her there, but it would be difficult. She'd planned carefully for weeks to ensure her tracks would be covered. She stared at the phone. So far it was the only thing that occupied the oversized old desk, and when it rang it had looked as dangerous as a coiled rattler.

She smiled. Thank heavens her viper had turned into a garden snake.

Emma Weathers arrived just as Samantha had loaded her arms with books and climbed atop the sturdy old desk to reach the top shelf of the bookcase.

"Ms. Delaney?" a voice called from the other room. "It's Emma Weathers."

"Just a minute. I'm coming." She shifted the armload of books and wondered how to best get down without breaking her neck or dropping the books.

"See? I'm needed already."

She looked down to find the smiling face of Emma Weathers. A petite brunette with curly shoulder-length hair and a ready smile, her appearance suited her voice.

Samantha laughed. "I can't argue with that."

Emma set her résumé down, scrambled into the office chair, and eased some of the books from Samantha's arms. Samantha deposited the rest on the shelf and climbed down.

She brushed off her hands and shook Emma's.

"Thank you. I'll bet that's the strangest beginning to a job interview that you've ever had."

"Actually, yes." Emma laughed. "I hope you didn't mind my coming on in, but the door was ajar."

Samantha mentally admonished herself for being so careless. She'd forgotten to lock the door behind her after carrying in the last of the boxes. The thunderstorms of two days earlier were long ago, the sun was shining in a clear blue sky, and she was finally getting her life in order. It was all too easy, at least on such a beautiful fall morning, to believe she was no longer in danger. Easy but foolish.

She wouldn't be that careless again.

"No, no problem. Is this your résumé?" Samantha lifted the paper and scanned Emma's qualifications. As she'd hoped, Emma was more than qualified for the job. "The hours are few, but my schedule—and yours—would be extremely flexible." She shrugged. "I'm afraid that's one of the few perks I have to woo you with."

"Well, with two kids that's the best one I can think of."

"In that case, how would you feel about taking the job on a trial basis?"

"Great. When would you like for me to start?"

Samantha glanced at the chaos around them.

"Today, huh?"

It took a moment for the meaning of Emma's words to sink in. "Really? You wouldn't mind?"

"Not at all. I have a few errands to run, then I'll be

back." She put her hands on her hips and looked from the boxes to the empty desk. "We've got work to do."

Daniel watched Emma Weathers's car pull out of the drive. After it was gone, he dropped a heavy bundle of roofing into the bed of the pickup truck and shoved it against the back of the rusted cab. What the hell did Emma want with Samantha? He'd long ago forgiven her for turning her back on him after the fire. She'd practically been a kid. Hell, she'd only done what the rest of the town had done.

Still, seeing Emma always caused a sharp prick of resentment. Back then he'd thought they were friends, if not something more. He retrieved another bundle of roofing from the storage shed and dropped it into the bed of the pickup truck. Who could blame her? Her family had been dirt poor, and she had wanted something more for herself. She'd wanted the mayor's son, not a man turned old too soon with a future full of troubles, not the bright promise he'd expected.

But things turned out the way they were supposed to. Emma had married Gus Weathers, and they'd inherited Gus's father's hardware store a few years back. Gus was a decent guy, but lately looked as if he carried the weight of the world on his shoulders.

Daniel had been in the store recently, and seen that Gus's hair was more white than brown, his thin shoulders stooped as he stocked the shelves. He was the spitting image of his father, but old Mr. Weathers had always been quick with a smile and a handshake. Gus, on the other hand, looked miserable.

Daniel hadn't seen Emma in ages. It might not be his place, but he intended to find out what business she had with Samantha. He felt a pang of guilt, then a strange sense of anticipation. Samantha's brown eyes had gone from warm to sizzling with anger the previous morning. Anger. He almost felt relieved to know he was still capable of rousing emotion of any kind in a woman.

It wouldn't have killed him to drive her to the sheriff's office, but that would have meant pretending he didn't know what had happened on that rain-slicked road two nights ago.

And he did.

Deception wasn't something he was comfortable with, though his mother had forced him to live a lie for years, where David was concerned. But in all other aspects of his life he'd embraced the truth, no matter how brutal. It was a necessary balance to his mother's lies, painful but reliable.

He allowed himself an indulgent moment as he imagined Samantha, anger intact, her slender body coiled with tension, dark eyes flashing sparks of gold. Suddenly he was sorry she hadn't lost her temper. He ran the callused palms of his hands across the rough surface of the pickup's tailgate. Feeling anything for Samantha Delaney was dangerous, and what he was feeling was insane. He barely knew her, but he knew enough. She was the last complication he needed right now.

He could tell her the truth about her accident two nights ago, but it was anybody's guess how she'd react. Packing up and leaving was one possibility, and as hard-hearted as it seemed, even to him, he needed the money. Besides, the thought of reintroducing David to the community left him cold, and the idea of Francis being the first to know was enough to make him physically sick.

He wouldn't keep David locked up like a prisoner, though. His brother had been a prisoner too long already. When the time was right, he would take that final step. But not until then. He was in control now. He slammed the tailgate shut and slid into the cab.

And he intended to find out what Samantha Delaney was up to.

Just as he pulled up to the back of the mansion, Samantha walked around the corner. Dressed in a plain T-shirt and gray sweatpants, she almost looked like a kid. Almost. The white T-shirt, covered liberally with smudges of dust, outlined her breasts and small waistline, and the baggy sweatpants only hinted at the slender hips underneath.

Daniel opened the door and stepped out of the truck.

"I need you to do something for me," she stated before he could greet her.

"Sure. What—"

"I've bought a dead bolt lock. Would you mind installing it on the interior door of the house?"

She was afraid? The thought hadn't crossed his mind. Then it hit him. There was a dead bolt lock on the main entrance to the house, and he was the only other person with a key. She was afraid of him. He looked at Samantha, at the childlike ponytail that was slightly askew, her thin arms and hands. He literally towered over her, his body easily twice as large as hers.

She extended a plastic-encased dead bolt kit. As he took it from her he noticed that one corner had been opened and the set of keys removed. She was in a strange place. She didn't know him. Of course she had every reason to be cautious. But the thought brought an odd mixture of anger and disappointment.

His gaze returned, not for the first time since they'd met, to the ring finger of her right hand. An engagement ring. The diamond was of a generous size, the cut classic. An odd pain gripped his chest. She'd marked "single" on the rental form, but then again she'd failed, probably intentionally, to make it clear that Sam Delaney was Samantha Delaney. Female. Still, she wore the ring on her right hand instead of her left. And there was no wedding band.

It occurred to him, then, that he probably knew less about Samantha Delaney than she did about him.

He met her gaze and nodded. "I'll do it today."

"Thanks."

"Samantha." He caught her arm as she started to walk away, the heat of her skin coaxing his fingers to linger.

She looked up at him, and for a moment he saw in her eyes a flash of something he hadn't seen in years. Interest. And desire?

"Is anything wrong?"

She hesitated, then the corners of her mouth lifted slightly in a smile. "No."

Just "no," he noticed. No explanation, no reassuring words. Well, what did he expect? Her gaze darted to his hand, and he felt his breath catch as he realized his thumb was stroking the soft skin of her upper arm. He dropped his hand as if he'd been burned.

"Are you afraid?" he asked.

He felt the tension enter her body, though they no longer touched. She raised her chin and met his eyes. "Yes."

At her answer Samantha watched various emotions play across Daniel's tanned face. The muscles of his jaw flexed beneath high cheekbones as he leaned closer. "Are you afraid of me?"

The question was almost a whisper, but his eyes were infused with something unreadable. It was part challenge, part invitation, she realized. The question itself stopped her short too. Afraid of him? It was almost funny. The only thing that frightened her about Daniel Caldwell was the way he made her forget all reason whenever he was close. Like now.

Every line in his body was drawn tight with frustration, with anticipation. Samantha had never been a physical person, didn't find it easy to hug or reach out to another person, but she had the sudden urge to soothe him, to convince him he'd misunderstood. Her hand reached for his as if of its own accord, and the contact of her fingertips against his startled her. In an instant he entwined his fingers with hers.

"Of course not." Her breath caught in her chest

and she dropped his hand. "I have no reason to be afraid of you."

"Then why?"

Samantha looked down at the ground. She hadn't trusted anyone except the state prosecutor with the knowledge of her whereabouts, and she'd barely convinced herself to tell him about the death threats. She didn't know whom she could trust. DiCarlo's influence was far-reaching, and his pockets were deep. Still, she'd come to Daniel's home, possibly endangering him as well. He deserved to know the truth. There was more to it than that, though. She wanted—needed—to tell him.

"You've never asked why I'm here."

Daniel slid his hands into the front pockets of his jeans. His expression was neutral, but his eyes held concern. "I figured that was your business. Are you in some kind of trouble?"

She laughed. She hadn't meant to, but the sound escaped before she could stop it. "Some kind of trouble" was such an understatement that she hardly knew where to begin. "Yes, in a manner of speaking." She paused. "I'm a document verification expert and—"

"I thought you were a writer." Daniel's brow furrowed in confusion. "That's what you put on the rental application."

"I am. I'm working on a book, one that combines the science of document verification and graphology." She waved her hand as she saw a look of total confusion come over his face. "Graphology determines personality traits through handwriting, and document verification is a scientific process that determines who a handwriting sample belongs to."

"I'll take your word for it."

She nodded. "Well, have you ever heard of Dante DiCarlo?"

His eyebrows raised in surprise. "Who hasn't?"

"He's going on trial next month. I've been called in as a handwriting expert to testify that he forged his partner's signature on legal documents."

"His dead partner."

She nodded again. "Yes. And to make a long story short, he's been threatening me."

Daniel straightened, every muscle in his body suddenly tense. "Did you tell the authorities?"

"The first time, I did. But DiCarlo is clever. He's been sending faxed messages, untraceable of course. All the messages came from telephone lines in out-of-state hotels." She shrugged. "By the time they compiled enough information to do anything about it, the trial would be over or I would be dead. Or both."

She said the words so easily. Daniel found himself staring at her, totally dumbfounded. She was feminine and beautiful, tiny and vulnerable. But she was also brave and determined. He watched as she rubbed her upper arms, exposed to the chill fall air beneath her shirtsleeves. She was trembling.

He wanted to pull her into his embrace, hold her head against his chest. He wanted to reassure her that she was safe. Hell, that was only part of it. He wanted to touch her. Wanted it more than he could recall wanting anything in a long time.

"So that's why you're here?" he asked.

"A s-safe place until the t-trial."

She was shivering uncontrollably now, her teeth chattering so that she hardly got the last words out. Daniel stepped forward and drew her against his chest. She didn't resist. Instead she allowed herself to be held against him, the curves of her body fitting perfectly against his. He closed his eyes. It defied all reason, taking a total stranger in his arms, but he was powerless to resist the need.

"You're trembling," he whispered against her ear.

She smelled faintly like a blend of citrus and flowers. No perfume, just a touch of shampoo and powder. He breathed in the scent of her, relishing the crash of sensations long denied. Then his body began to stir, and he stepped back. The separation was as painful as pulling a bandage from an unhealed wound. He realized, then, that he had needed to hold Samantha Delaney as much as she'd needed to be held.

Probably more.

She looked up and met his gaze. Her eyes had softened to a warm shade of brown, the expression on her face a mixture of desire and embarrassment.

"Let's get you inside." He pressed his hand between her shoulder blades and willed his body to ignore her nearness. "And I'll get this lock installed."

The low-growing branch of the dogwood tree blocked the view of Samantha and Daniel, but one quick snap took care of that. *So this was how it was.* The two of them were together. Cold fury turned into red-hot anger as they slipped inside the house together. She thought he would protect her. How noble.

"Enjoy your time, Samantha." The tiny dogwood sapling was snapped at the base this time, just for the sheer satisfaction of it. "You don't have long."

Just before she closed the front door behind her and Daniel, Samantha glanced around the small front yard. She'd had the distinct feeling that someone was there . . . watching them. The quiet two-lane road that ran directly in front of the house turned into Main Street a few blocks down, giving way to the town's business district. At the moment it was empty, with the exception of a pair of children on bicycles. She watched one, then the other, pop a wheelie before dissolving into laughter. It was beautiful here. Scottsdale was the picture-postcard image of a small southern town. So why did she have the feeling that danger had found her? She rubbed the chill from her arms and closed the door.

When she turned, she found herself facing Daniel's chest.

"Is everything all right?" His voice was low and the look on his face told her that he'd noticed her nervous glance outside.

"Yes." The yellow glow of the foyer's chandelier cast an intimate light, shutting out the rest of the world while seeming to draw them into one of their own. His eyes were piercing, looking at her with the same intensity she'd seen the night he pulled her from the sheriff's car.

She rubbed frantically at her upper arms before stepping around him. "I was expecting someone."

"Emma Weathers?"

Daniel's voice stopped her cold. It was a simple question, but his words were infused with something more. Accusation? She shook her head. Paranoia was overcoming her.

She met his even stare. "Yes. How did you know?"

"Scottsdale's a small town." A sideways smile lit his face. "I saw her pulling out of the drive earlier."

"Then I hope you approve." She paused to examine the amused expression that came over his face. "I've hired her to work as my assistant—part-time—while I'm here."

He ripped the heavy plastic from the dead bolt. "I'm sure she'll do fine."

"So you do know her then?"

His expression neutral, he slowly unbuttoned his flannel shirt. "Almost all my life." He shrugged out of the shirt.

Samantha felt her body go rigid. Daniel Caldwell was gorgeous. And to top it off, he apparently had no idea. A white T-shirt covered his wide chest, its short sleeves accentuating the hard muscles of his tanned upper arms, while well-defined forearms hinted that he worked with his hands. She recalled the way he'd deftly handled the power saw.

She also recalled the way he'd deftly dismissed her. "What do you do for a living?" The question sounded stark and impolite in the empty foyer, not to mention the awkward silence that followed.

Finally he turned to face her, and her breath caught in her throat. The expression in his eyes was almost angry, but she felt a tremor of excitement run through her. He twisted the flannel shirt in his fists, looking as if he wanted to punch the heavy plaster wall. He also looked as if he might cross the foyer and kiss her.

Illogically, she took a step closer.

Daniel walked toward her as well, until they were only inches apart. She wanted to reach for him, aching to touch the dark blond hair that fell against his collar, to run her fingertips across the soft cotton of his T-shirt, to feel the muscles of his chest move beneath the fabric. . . .

He wrapped the flannel shirt around her shoulders. "Here," he whispered. "I'll bet you're still freezing."

She stifled a hysterical laugh. The warm sensation that was pulsing through her left her anything but cold. Daniel's nearness had stolen that from her since they first touched in the courtyard. She eased her arms into the flannel. The scent of him surrounded her, and the warmth from his skin that lingered on the fabric made her literally dizzy with desire.

She closed her eyes and allowed the feeling to fully enter her. Desire. When was the last time she'd wanted a man? Suddenly she wasn't sure she ever had. At least, nothing she'd ever felt for another man could compare to the illogical desire Daniel Caldwell could stir in her with an innocent touch.

"What do I do for a living?" His voice was low and sultry. "I'm your landlord, remember?"

She opened her eyes. "I remember," she whispered. "Was that the wrong question to ask?"

He shook his head. "Not as long as you're the one asking."

"Then what else do you do?"

"I fix things." He slipped his hand behind her neck, his callused palm scattering fresh chill bumps down her arms. "Do you have anything that needs fixing?"

She bit her lip, forcing the raw emotion to remain at bay. "Just my life."

He eased her hair over the collar of the shirt, then tugged the flannel into place. "I'll see what I can do."

FIVE

Daniel added a second stick of kindling to the fire and nudged the fading embers to life with the poker. Glancing at his brother, he searched for a reaction. There wasn't one.

Instead, David sat on the edge of the worn sofa, staring at the empty easel. His hands twitched with excitement, but he seemed to barely notice the flames that crackled and popped just a few feet away.

Daniel propped the iron poker against the hearth. Why had he built the fire? It was hardly cold enough outside to need one, and the small living room was already so warm that he'd been forced to crack a window to allow some cool air to circulate. Of course he knew the answer. He'd wanted to gauge David's reaction, to see if his brother had some morbid fascination with fire.

He shook his head. Thirteen years and he still

couldn't convince himself that David had been responsible.

A luna moth hit the window screen, its massive body thumping wildly against the mesh as it was drawn toward the flames. No lights were on in the small room, and the iridescent green of the moth's wings reflected the firelight as it tried in vain to reach the thing that could destroy it.

It was late in the season for the insect. Daniel watched its frantic, determined flailing before closing his eyes to the sight. He was like that moth, he realized. Trying desperately to catch up to his own life . . . and drawn toward Samantha despite himself, despite the danger.

In his mind he saw her face, pale and frightened, as she'd described the threats Dante DiCarlo had made. He felt the muscles in his forearms twitch with tension, and realized he'd balled his hands into fists. He had a feeling Samantha Delaney didn't scare easily. But she was certainly frightened now.

"Is it time to paint?" David's voice penetrated his thoughts.

Daniel looked at his brother. Tonight he didn't have to disappoint David. He crossed the living room to the kitchen and returned with paintbrushes, a few tubes of oils, a mason jar filled with turpentine, and two yellowed canvas boards that had seen better days.

You could pick up just about anything you needed in Gus Weathers's hardware store—anything from roofing nails to a loaf of bread. Lord knows he'd bought his share of roofing nails and house paint there over the years, but somehow he'd managed to ignore the sparsely stocked dusty corner that held art supplies. That afternoon, however, he'd scooped up a few tubes of oils and had rummaged through the cheap canvas boards until he found two that were only moderately warped.

He smiled. The hardware store wisely stocked enough art supplies to keep the local high school's art teacher happy, and enough crib notes to give the English teacher high blood pressure.

Daniel recalled, with less enthusiasm, Gus's measured reaction as he'd rung up the items. It wasn't in Gus Weathers's nature to comment, but his eyes had held curiosity. It was common knowledge that Daniel had been a talented artist in his youth. Everyone had expected him to pursue his art, and the fact that he hadn't was probably looked upon as yet another Caldwell tragedy. He could just see the good citizens of Scottsdale shaking their heads with sympathy while they passed along this latest piece of gossip about the last Caldwell.

It turned his stomach. His name had been synonymous with "such a tragedy" for longer than he cared to remember.

Daniel shook off the melancholy thoughts as he faced the unabashed eagerness in his brother's eyes. With a theatrical sweep of his hand he presented the items to David. "Tonight we paint."

But his brother didn't reach for the tubes of paint as Daniel imagined he would. Instead he sat perfectly still, waiting. Then it hit him. David had never painted alone. He'd always tagged along, painting in the shadows of the attic, imitating the delicate touch of Daniel's brush with his own broad strokes and abstract interpretation.

"Me first, huh?"

David nodded.

His brother's expression was thoughtful, but his silence opened the door to doubt. It had been that way for as long as Daniel could recall. It was as if David were a nocturnal observer of life, always on the edge of living in the same world as others and too caught up in his own thoughts to communicate in sentences of more than two or three words.

Well, so be it. Tonight they would recapture some of the magic they'd shared as children. As brothers.

He stepped up to the canvas with well-planned enthusiasm and an expression that he hoped belied the fact that he hadn't picked up a paintbrush in over a decade. His fingers trembled as he uncapped the first tube. Red. He'd managed to find red, black, white, and yellow. No blue. He wiped perspiration from his brow. Gus really should have stocked more blue. He felt his pulse pounding against his temples as a blob of red met the aluminum pie plate he'd found to use as a makeshift palette.

This was ridiculous. He was approaching the simple act of painting like a virgin schoolboy on his first date. There were no judge and jury for what he was about to do. No one looking at him except David. And David, bless him, would probably watch him with as much reverence as one would watch Michelangelo. He always had.

He dipped his brush and stroked the color against the canvas with more determination than finesse. His chest constricted. He dipped the brush a second time and mentally cursed his shaking hand as it left a clumsy streak of red against the canvas. He never knew what he was going to paint until the image emerged in his head. For now, all he knew was that red was the right choice.

He dipped and stroked a third time. Something tight unlocked within him. More color. Yes, that was right. Cover the entire canvas. Background. That was right. Behind him he could hear David shuffling. He glanced over his shoulder. His brother had torn the thin plastic from the second canvas and was staring at him. Good. Daniel could tell by the expression on David's face that he was pleased. He didn't urge him to join in. That would happen, as it always had, when David was ready.

Smooth. Now the brush occasionally met the previous stroke, blending the smooth oil over the canvas, scumbling the dime-store purchase with color and life. Again and again.

David's hand appeared next to his, stealing a paintbrush that rested against the easel's tray, then dipping it in the red paint like a mischievous thief. The years melted away. The pain, the loss were absorbed in the mindless pleasure of the task.

His mind drifted as he worked. Samantha. Warm brown eyes that could melt the coldest heart, enough fire in that auburn hair to tempt a man to touch it. Daniel shook his head. She'd started out as an unwanted, unneeded distraction but was becoming something else entirely. When he wasn't watching for her, he was thinking about her. How many times had he glanced toward the house, wondering if she was there, what she was doing?

And yesterday . . . yesterday he'd held her. Only for a moment and under the pretense of comforting her. But he thought he'd felt her sigh, felt her body press lightly against his in a sweet, hesitant invitation.

Daniel opened the tube of black and squeezed a portion of it next to the red on the palette, then blended the two to match the shade in his head. He stroked the darker color in a hasty pattern, preparing the background for the object that would soon appear, first in his mind, then on the canvas.

His thoughts scattered again as he worked. Samantha had fixed them each a mug of hot cocoa and watched him from the staircase as he installed the dead bolt lock on her door. She hadn't seemed angry or embarrassed by the physical affection that had passed between them, just comfortable with the lack of conversation and willing to pass time with him. The paintbrush paused above the swirl of paint. With *him*.

For some reason he'd found it hard to ask her about Emma Weathers. It was as if he were afraid she'd sensed the old connection he and Emma had once shared. But if she did, or if Emma had told her, she didn't react. Instead, once he managed to ask why Emma had been there, she had talked about Emma's qualifications and how lucky she felt to find her. Daniel pushed at a strand of hair that was annoying him, feeling a blob of paint smudge his forehead. Maybe having Emma around would be good for Samantha, given what she was experiencing. If that was the case, he was more than willing to tolerate any awkward moments that might pass between him and Emma.

Emma would have left his mind long ago if not for the way she'd behaved after the fire. They'd shared just one summer together as lovers. He'd been home from college and she'd been there waiting. Young and vulnerable, Emma had represented the innocence and acceptance of his hometown, chasing away the uncertainty he'd felt at school. She'd become part of the pain, though, after the fire, another soul who had turned her back on him. Long ago forgiven but never forgotten.

Daniel stepped back from the canvas and eyed his progress. Cadmium red formed the background, melding to a deeper, darker shade in the center. He cocked his head, willing the right image to form. In a single motion he pulled off his T-shirt and wrapped the worn material over his right hand, then wiped out the area where the features should be. His hand darted over the canvas. Quickly, before the image faded. He tugged the soft cotton tightly over his index finger, concentrating on the detail of the eyes and mouth, then scrubbing away the paint until the lighter area of the cheekbones and forehead formed.

Eventually a shaded image appeared where earlier only the smoky maroon had existed, a sort of hazy blueprint of the face he knew would soon fully form. His shoulders cramped, his knees felt frozen into place as he worked. Red, yellow, and white swirled together against the canvas. He balled his fist in frustration. The flesh tones weren't right.

At some point the fire had died, because the pungent odor of cold ashes now drifted from the fireplace. He could tell the room was cooler, yet beads of perspiration trickled down his bare chest, eventually meeting the waistband of his jeans.

Finally, he dipped his brush for the last time, knowing fatigue was winning over perfection. The tip of the brush touched golden-brown to one eye, then the other. That was almost right. He squinted at the detail, maddeningly impossible and not intended for the cheap, rough canvas. Still, it was close. The highlight of brown eyes flashing with emotion, with passion for life.

Finally, he closed his own eyes and stepped back. When he opened them again, the imperfect image of a woman stared back at him. Samantha. Hadn't he known it would be when his hand first lifted the brush? Almost as an afterthought, he leaned down and initialed the lower corner in black.

He glanced over his shoulder at David, who had pulled a footstool behind the easel and was sitting atop it, cross-legged, the cheap board-backed canvas resting against his knees. He was totally immersed in what he was working on, so much so that he didn't pause when Daniel stepped behind him.

Daniel looked down at the canvas and felt the room

spin. He knelt down beside his brother, as much to steady his own legs as to examine the painting. Why?

Why had David chosen to create something so horrible?

Beside him, his brother was still working fervently, busy completing the image that dominated the canvas. Daniel looked at the repulsive painting, then at the angelic smile on David's face. Good God, he thought. The colors were the same, even the off-center placement and casual pose mirrored his own portrait of Samantha.

But nothing—nothing—could have prepared him for the image of the woman that stared back at him.

Samantha laughed as the old-fashioned toaster sent the bread flying through the air. She caught it and tossed it onto the paper napkin before it burned her fingers. The old house was full of surprises, she'd learned. From the shower, which sometimes decided to pump only cold water, to the curious creaks and settling noises that she'd finally grown accustomed to. She shook her head. And now the toaster.

She spread butter and homemade pear preserves on the toast, then retrieved her now-favorite daisy mug from the cabinet and fixed a cup of hot tea. The preserves had been purchased at a quaint little gift shop that sold only homemade goods. She'd always heard that the town of Scottsdale did a booming craft-and-antiques business, but she hadn't expected the high volume of tourism.

On the few occasions she'd had to look around, she'd been charmed by the stores that lined Main Street, the old-fashioned soda shop that still catered to the local school children, and the hundred-year-old oak trees that seemed to spring from the sidewalks. There certainly wasn't much not to like about Scottsdale. With the exception of the local sheriff's office, she amended.

So far she'd stopped by the sheriff's office twice, and on both occasions Francis Smitherman had conveniently been out. The first time she'd bought the story, but the second time a pair of shiny black boots had been visible from his office doorway, propped lazily on an empty oak desk. That, along with the lingering smell of onion rings and barbecue, had left her suspicious.

Today she didn't plan on calling ahead. First she would do some sightseeing and antiquing, along with the other city folks who had made the drive from Atlanta that weekend, then she'd drop in, unannounced, to pay a visit with Sheriff Smitherman.

She was determined to learn if anyone had reported a missing person, an accident, anything that could be linked to the person she'd hit.

Her gaze automatically shifted to the window before she carried her toast and tea to the kitchen table. She made a growling noise of disgust. When was she going to stop wondering where Daniel was every minute of every day?

Several days had passed since he'd installed the dead bolt lock, and she'd rarely seen him since. She took a sip of tea. As much as she hated to admit it, that fact disappointed her. Something had passed between them that afternoon. She would have to be dead not to feel it. But apparently Daniel had chosen to ignore it . . . and her.

The remainder of the week had passed in a flash, though, with Emma dropping by during school hours to help her organize the office. Finally the jumble of manuscript binders and research books had been arranged in workable order. Her small computer was waiting for her atop the old desk, and the fax machine was plugged in and ready to handle the few clients she planned to work with during her hiatus. Samantha bit the corner of her toast and closed her eyes with pleasure. She made a mental note to drop by the gift shop for more preserves.

It had taken time and all the strength she could muster, but she was beginning to relax in the apartment. In fact, she hadn't looked over her shoulder or inspected the shadows in the last twenty-four hours. Now that, she figured, deserved a celebration. She finished the toast in a flash and carried the mug to the sink. Now it was time for her reward—a weekend of mindless shopping.

In less than five minutes, Samantha was pulling her car into one of the few parking places left along Main Street. The merchants had prepared for the tourists, hanging brightly colored quilts and displaying local crafts outside the tiny shops. Baby strollers bumped along the uneven sidewalks, and laughter blended with the hum of shoppers' voices, penetrating the otherwise still morning. The slant of the autumn sun lit the little town like a diamond under glass.

Several antebellum homes along Main Street had been restored to their former glory, one providing a stately home for law offices, another used as the local museum. She thought of the Caldwell home, just blocks away, which was clinging to its former beauty by a thread. Not a day passed when Daniel wasn't making repairs to the house, but it seemed time and mother nature was always a step ahead of him.

She slipped into the first antique shop that wasn't overrun with customers. Inside, an older man looked up from the cash register and greeted her with a cheerful smile.

"Hi there." He waved his hand toward the interior of the shop before sliding his glasses back into place and taking a screwdriver to the cash register's drawer. "Make yourself at home and give a yell if you need . . ." His voice drifted off as he returned his attention to the task of repairing the cash register.

"Thank you."

Samantha was instantly lost in the array of antiques that haphazardly lined the shelves and walls of the tiny shop. The aroma of scented candles mixed with the musty smell of the old building and the antiques that filled the place. She stopped to run her fingers across an iron statue of a horse, brushing away the thick dust that clung to her finger.

Antique shops in Atlanta were selective, acquiring only the best, then displaying their treasures in the most alluring fashion, the old wood of furniture polished to a mirror's sheen, more personal items displayed in charming scenarios next to freshly cut flowers. But in Scottsdale, it seemed, it was up to the buyer to separate junk from treasure, to decide for oneself what was valuable.

Samantha drifted toward a wall of paintings. Some were obviously antiques, others probably local artists' work. Most were quite good, others more amateurish in style. But one painting stopped her dead. It was a beautiful oil of the Caldwell mansion. Or at least it appeared to be. She backed up to get a better view. The painting was large, and the heavy gilded frame that held it made the work even larger.

In the painting, frothy pink azaleas lined a well-manicured lawn. The house shone bright white, an American flag captured slightly adrift in a breeze. The work must have been done years ago, she realized. Before the house fell into disrepair.

She raised on tiptoe to be seen over a tall shelf. "Excuse me," she called. "How much are you asking for this oil?"

The older man slid his bifocals into place and glanced at the wall. He paused for a moment before answering. "I'm asking two hundred and fifty for that one. Did you notice that frame? The picture isn't an antique, but the frame is."

A shiver of excitement ran through her. That picture belonged at the Caldwell place, belonged with Daniel. She knew, in that instant, that she'd buy it for him. How she was going to talk him into accepting it, she didn't know. She smiled. She'd cross that bridge later.

"I'll take it," she called over the display.

"Great. I'll just go in the back and get the ladder," the man said over his shoulder as he disappeared into a room behind the counter.

Samantha drifted toward the cash register, only halfheartedly admiring the other antiques.

In a minute the proprietor shuffled back to the front, tugging a step ladder behind him.

She drew her billfold out of her purse and waited while he propped the ladder against the wall. "The painting is of Daniel Caldwell's house, isn't it?"

The man's gaze snapped to her, and for a moment she thought a look of recognition crossed his face. She noticed his fingers trembled as he adjusted his glasses again. "Oh." He paused. "You meant *that* painting."

Samantha glanced at the wall where the paintings were hung, searching for one remotely similar to the one she'd picked out. "The biggest oil painting, the one of the antebellum home—"

The man abruptly turned and carried the ladder back into the storage room. "I'm sorry. I misunderstood," he called from the other room. "That one's not for sale."

Disappointment, then curiosity, surged through her. He *hadn't* misunderstood her. She was certain of it. She picked up a yellowed business card from the acrylic holder that sat atop the counter. "If you change your mind"—she glanced at the card—"Mr. Moses, I would love to buy it."

Leonard Moses didn't respond as he returned to the front room. Standing behind the counter, he kept his head down and unnecessarily shuffled paperwork. She made him nervous, she thought. But why? She walked back to the wall of paintings and examined the artwork a second time. It was, without a doubt, the Caldwell place. The image was exact, right down to the gaslight that bordered the stairs and the porthole next to the entrance door. She cocked her head and examined the lower right corner. The initials *D.C.* were cleverly worked into the pattern of the grass.

D.C. for Daniel Caldwell? She envisioned Daniel's hands, callused and weatherworn from hard work. In her mind, though, she could imagine those same hands holding the delicate stem of a paintbrush, creating the image of his house with the same loving care he now used to try to salvage it.

Turning, she cleared her throat. "My name is Samantha Delaney and I'm staying at the Caldwell place." She watched Leonard Moses's face, waiting for some look of surprise. There wasn't any. Finally, she slid the business card inside her purse. "As I said, I'd love to buy the painting if you change your mind."

The old man met her eyes and nodded in a gesture of dismissal. "I'll keep that in mind, Miss Delaney."

"She *what*?" Daniel remembered to lower his voice, casting a quick glance toward the bedroom where David was sleeping.

Moses paced the floor of the guest cottage with

short nervous steps. "Hell, I didn't know what to do. I didn't even realize who she was until the last minute."

Daniel found that difficult to imagine. Samantha was the most striking woman to grace the streets of Scottsdale in ages. Probably ever. His eyes narrowed in suspicion as Moses stopped in front of him. "Are you drinking again?"

The guilty expression that crossed the older man's face told the whole story. The answer was yes, and Daniel knew the excuses would soon pour from him if he didn't put a stop to it.

He threw his hand up. "Sorry. That's your business."

Moses's gaze met his. Clear blue eyes twinkled with stubbornness and a bit of childish mischief. "Your darn tootin' it is."

He felt a part of him soften, as it always did with Moses. He rubbed his hands across his face. "So how much money did I almost make?"

"Two hundred and fifty dollars."

Daniel's eyebrows shot up. Samantha had been willing to pay that kind of money for a portrait of his family home? He'd long ago written the painting's value off as merely sentimental. It had been hanging, unnoticed, in Moses's shop for years. Well, sentimental or not, two hundred and fifty dollars would have just about covered the roofing shingles he'd bought last week.

"Should I have let her buy it?" Moses's gaze searched his. Undoubtedly the older man sensed his disappointment over the money. "You've always been so darned private about your painting." He pulled his glasses off and began to wipe them repeatedly. "I was confused. Didn't know what to do."

The liquor always confuses you, Daniel thought. Finally, he shook his head. "No. Sooner or later she'd have noticed the initials and started asking questions." The image of David's painting flashed in his head. "That's the last thing I want right now."

Moses replaced his glasses, then pointed toward the window. "She's home. The light just went on."

Daniel turned to look. Through the boarded attic window shone slants of light. "Oh my God."

"What—"

Without answering, Daniel ran to David's room. It was empty, the bed a tangle of sheets and bedspread. He pressed a reassuring hand to Moses's shoulder. "Stay here and wait for me. That's the attic light. I think David is in the house."

"How did he do it this time?" Moses ran to the window and looked up at the mansion. "I swear, that boy—"

Daniel followed his friend's gaze. Washed in moonlight, the house looked like an old, willful woman. But it held more than secrets and temptation that night.

"What about Samantha?"

Daniel's gaze fell on Samantha's car in the driveway, and his heart turned to ice. She was home. On impulse he ran to the dining room. His painting still rested on the easel. But David's was gone.

What about Samantha? Moses's words echoed in his head as he flung open the front door and ran toward the mansion. His thoughts raced faster than he could will his legs to move. Samantha—frightened and alone. David—the painting. An image of the painting flashed in Daniel's mind. Why had David taken it with him?

The painting had been, he supposed, of Samantha—a replica of his own work no doubt. But the image had been twisted, altered. In David's work, Samantha's face had been a brushstroked collage of flesh and ashes, the tips of her hair curled into flames. But the worst, by far, had been her eyes. Empty sockets of black. Devoid of color, devoid of life.

My God, Daniel thought as he reached the porch, what had made him paint her that way? He'd trusted—believed in—his brother when no one else had. Was David capable of hurting her? The truth was, he didn't know.

And he didn't intend to find out.

He opened the front door. "Samantha?" The word was out before he could form a plan, before he considered the possibility of finding David without alerting Samantha.

No one answered.

He stopped in the dark foyer and listened. There were no sounds besides the rhythmic ticking of the grandfather clock from inside Samantha's apartment. Daniel felt a terror he hadn't known in thirteen years.

"David." The word was a half whisper, a half-angry demand for a response.

From upstairs a heavy thump sounded. Direction. He finally had direction. Adrenaline pumped through his body as he took the stairs two at a time. The attic door was already ajar when he reached the top. He clenched his teeth, fighting the terrifying scenarios that were running through his mind.

As he stepped through the door, David turned toward him and smiled. Barefoot and clad in only a loose button-front shirt and boxer shorts, he held the painting against his chest, the image facing outward. The contrast between his brother's innocent smile and the diabolical portrait was staggering.

"Needs to dry," David said simply.

Daniel tore his gaze from David's painting and searched the attic for Samantha. His eyes struggled to adjust to the shadowy room, lit only by the moonlight that slanted through the boarded window. He crossed to the center of the attic and found the chain for the single lightbulb that hung overhead. As he pulled it, David stepped farther into the shadows that lined the attic.

Daniel visually searched every corner of the room for Samantha. Finally he took a deep breath. There was no sign of her. He felt a sagging relief as he realized his brother was alone.

But then David propped the painting against a wall, the abstract, macabre likeness and the vacant eyes reminding him that Samantha could still be in danger. Or worse.

"Leave it here." Daniel heard the stern tone of his own voice and watched David's face draw into a frown of confusion.

Then he understood. They had always painted in the attic and had always left the canvases there, beyond the critical eyes of their parents. But the room had been different then—semifurnished, with working windows and filled with gentle breezes and sunlight. Now the windows were boarded, shadows and moisture creeping into the corners and nooks.

Daniel looked at his brother. An even spattering of brown hair covered his arms and legs, and his face was a handsome mix of innocence and maturity. Not only was the attic different, they were different.

Daniel slowly crossed the room and pressed his hand against his brother's shoulder. "We need to go home now," he said evenly. He realized that he sounded like the doctors and orderlies who had cared for David in the hospital, speaking in a hushed, careful tone as if he would shatter if spoken to like a capable adult. Daniel felt his stomach turn. He'd sworn never to talk to David like that.

But right now he didn't have the luxury of chance. The unnatural quiet of Samantha's apartment was playing in his mind like a scream for help. *Get David out. Check on Samantha. Hurry.* His own mind repeated the commands over and over. He gently pushed David forward, and to his relief his brother headed for the stairs.

Moses was waiting for them in the courtyard. "Samantha?"

He met the older man's worried gaze and shook his head. "I don't know. Take David back to the guest house while I keep looking."

David resisted Moses's efforts to tug him forward. His feet planted firmly in one spot, he turned to face Daniel. "Something's wrong?" he asked.

Intelligence. His brother's eyes held intelligence . . . and now something more. Maturity. Socially, David wasn't like everyone else, but he was smart and capable. Daniel was certain of it. The muscles of his jaw ached, and he realized he was clenching his teeth. If only he was as certain that his brother wouldn't harm Samantha.

"Everything is fine, David. Go back to the house with Moses and wait for me. I'll be there soon."

He watched as Moses and David headed toward the guest house, then walked back to the mansion. He forced himself not to run, not wanting to alarm David.

Maybe he was overreacting where Samantha was concerned. David couldn't have been gone more than a few minutes. But why hadn't she answered when he called? If nothing else, the commotion of his running up the old hardwood stairs should have brought her into the foyer to investigate.

Daniel entered the house and lifted his hand to the door that separated Samantha's apartment from the foyer. He knocked twice. "Samantha?"

No answer.

He waited, listening to the sound of his own ragged breathing. "Samantha . . . it's Daniel." He forced himself to sound calm. "Are you there?"

He thought he heard the muffled sound of her voice. He cocked his head. Had it been a cry? That was enough. He was through waiting, doing the polite thing. Her privacy be damned.

Daniel turned the doorknob. It moved, unlocked. A quick glance at the dead bolt told him it hadn't been broken. But it also hadn't been used. He eased the door open and stepped inside. The apartment was dark, as if the night had fallen without notice.

He spotted her silhouette instantly, one hip cocked against the doorframe of her office, her back to him.

"Samantha?" He waited for some response. She didn't move. Something was wrong.

Finally she turned slightly to acknowledge his presence. When he came closer, he could see that she was trembling. He walked up behind her and touched her on the shoulder. To his surprise, she sagged against him, her back to his chest, her head resting on his shoulder. For an instant all he could think about was the warm contact of their bodies. The sweet scent of her assaulted his senses, opening the door to longings better off forgotten.

But something was wrong.

He forced himself to move and turned her toward him. She refused to look up. Instead she stared vacantly at a sheet of paper shaking violently in her hand.

"What is it?" He eased the paper from her fingers. "What's wrong?"

She didn't have to answer. All he needed to know was written on the paper.

SIX

I've missed you. The words were printed in thick block letters.

Daniel resisted the urge to crumple the paper in his fist, laying it facedown on the desk instead.

"It was there when I got home." Samantha nodded toward the fax machine. "He knows I'm here."

The words were simple but probably all too true. Daniel noticed shopping bags just inside the study door. It was as if she'd dropped them at her feet after finding the faxed message.

"I thought someone was in the house." She looked up, her eyes dark with terror in the shadowy room.

The single desk lamp lit the right side of her face, and Daniel could see the path her tears had taken. How long had she been standing there?

"Then I heard you call my name." She pressed her fingertips to her lips. "Thank God it was you."

He pulled her into his arms. For what, he wasn't

sure. Comfort? Of course. Something more? He wanted it, yet he couldn't allow himself. But he could hold her. . . .

Her lips brushed against his neck, tentative at first and then with confidence. He closed his eyes, desire coursing through him as he felt her mouth open, felt the slight touch of her tongue against his skin. When she pressed the palm of her hand to his cheek, he opened his eyes.

In his sweetest dreams he couldn't have imagined the look of desire on Samantha's face. Her fingers curled against his unshaven jaw, drawing him toward her. When their mouths met in a mutual hunger, Daniel's entire body stiffened with need. Every longing he'd held in check burst forth as he felt the sweet invitation of her lips against his.

His tongue sought and found hers, mating in rhythmic silence. He grasped her slender hips, pulling her hard against his arousal. A small cry escaped her, and the action tempted him to be inside her, to enter the hot slickness of her body the way he now entered her mouth with his tongue.

She pulled away from him, but her hand still rested on his cheek. "Make love to me, Daniel," she whispered.

His pulse pounded against his temples. Had she actually said those words? His head slumped down to her shoulder. Think, he told himself. He didn't want to think. His hips moved involuntarily against hers, his desire spiraling out of control as she matched his movements. To be inside her . . . to move within her and feel her respond. . . .

Daniel wrapped his arm around the back of her neck and pulled her mouth to his a final time.

Final. He knew it would have to be, because she was frightened. He'd seen the lingering fear mixed with passion in her eyes. He couldn't take her like that. Reluctantly he lifted his mouth from hers. They would make love when she was thinking clearly, when she needed more than comfort. He met her eyes and silently vowed he'd make her want him again. Soon.

And then there would be no stopping, no waiting.

"You don't mean what you're saying," he whispered. "You're only frightened."

Samantha froze. Part of her wanted to argue with him and part of her wanted to pull away in embarrassment. His arms were still around her, his arousal nestled firmly between her hips. She shifted her body slightly and he stepped away, as if suddenly realizing that his words and his body were saying different things. He wanted her but wasn't willing.

Reality crashed down around her, her thoughts hammering at her composure with every beat of her heart. One, two . . . Had she actually asked him to make love to her? She'd been so afraid. Three, four . . . Daniel was practically a stranger, and she'd been with a grand total of three men in her life. She felt fresh tears against her cheek. Five, six . . . And he'd said no. But why?

He could be married. The thought was almost a physical blow.

She placed her hands against his chest and pushed. Without thinking, she ran to the kitchen and flung open the window over the sink. The cool damp air rushed in and she inhaled, allowing it to fill her lungs. Closing her eyes, she willed the tears away. She wasn't angry with Daniel. He hadn't done anything wrong, except respond to her. Her mind filled with the sweet sensation of his body pressed against hers, his tongue filling her mouth with a promise of what their love-making would be like. . . .

"Samantha?" Daniel touched her shoulder.

She jumped, then froze again, aware that he was standing behind her. The embarrassment melted away, and all she could think of was the nearness of his body, the fact that his hips probably rested only inches from her own. Yes, she was frightened, terrified of DiCarlo. He had been right about that. But that had nothing to do with what she was feeling for Daniel Caldwell right now.

"I'm sorry," she whispered, surprised at the raspy sound of her voice.

"For what?" His hand slid from her shoulder to the back of her neck, making distracting circles against the taut muscles.

"I—I don't really know you." As soon as she spoke she found herself wishing she hadn't started down that road. The explanation was too hard, his touch too tempting. If only he would move his hand. Then she could think. She paused. "Are you married?" she finally blurted out.

He laughed. Chuckled softly at first, then actually

laughed. She turned toward him. He'd straightened, his head thrown back to reveal two rows of perfect white teeth. The only light in the tiny kitchen was from the study's lamp slanting through the doorway. She allowed herself to examine him for the instant he was unaware. The tanned skin of his arms and face accentuated his dark blond hair and made the green of his eyes so vibrant, they looked unreal. She also knew that gaze could pierce her through with intensity . . . and desire.

"What's so funny?"

He stopped laughing and met her gaze. His expression altered, going from amused to serious in an instant. "Nothing." His voice was soft, laced with bedroom laziness that made her knees weak. He shook his head. "I'm not married, Samantha."

The sound of her name on his lips was almost more than she could stand.

He reached for her right hand and pulled it almost to his lips. When he turned it slightly, her mother's wedding ring sparkled in the half-light of the kitchen. "What about you, Samantha?"

She stared at the ring as if seeing it for the first time. It had honestly never occurred to her that anyone would mistake it for her own. "My mother's." He continued to stare at her, waiting. "I'm alone," she finally answered, the words as honest as any she'd ever uttered.

"No, you're not." He pulled her fingers to his mouth, planting kisses against her knuckles. She trembled as his tongue gently probed the delicate skin next to the wedding ring. When his gaze lifted to meet hers, she saw the raw need in his eyes.

Why are you denying us? she wanted to ask. But pride wouldn't allow it. She'd allowed herself to be afraid of DiCarlo, given him her power. Then she'd turned to a stranger for comfort. And Lord knows she was willing to accept more than comfort from Daniel that night. But he wasn't willing to give it.

Weakness. She hated herself for it.

Samantha closed her eyes and willed the emptiness to return. It wouldn't. She felt her panic rise. At eighteen she'd lost her parents in a car accident. That year she'd perfected the technique. She grasped the edge of the sink behind her and tried again. Push the emotion away, allow the nothingness to enter. . . .

"Are you okay?" Daniel's voice penetrated the silence.

She opened her eyes and met his concerned gaze. No, she wasn't okay. He'd stolen something from her. He'd taken the emptiness.

"You should go now." The words sounded flat, harsh, even to her own ears. She brushed past him and headed toward the front door.

In a moment he joined her, his strong, warm fingers wrapping around her upper arm. She noticed he held the faxed message in his other hand. He tugged her to face him. "I'm taking this to Francis." His voice was confident, his eyes lit with an odd mixture of anger and concern. "I'll be by in the morning to check on you."

She nodded and looked away. "Thanks."

"Samantha." He waited until she met his gaze

again. "Lock the door behind me." His fingers stroked her arm, and he lowered his voice to a whisper. "It's going to be all right."

She didn't argue; she didn't have the words to explain. In her heart, though, she knew the truth. It wasn't going to be okay. And not because of DiCarlo.

Daniel had stolen the emptiness, and nothing would be the same again.

Is everything okay?

Daniel slammed the truck into park. What a lame thing to say to Samantha after what had almost passed between them. Yet he'd asked her that question two times each day since she'd received the fax.

The first morning when she answered her door, her eyes had been red-rimmed and her hair disheveled. But by the time he checked on her that evening, she'd seemed composed and confident, thanking him and dismissing him in one well-rehearsed sentence. In the four days that had passed since, he hadn't sensed any emotion in her at all. A familiar tension knotted his shoulders. He wasn't sure which was worse, her pain and distress or her chilly reserve.

He threw an old blanket over his and David's paintings and tucked them under his arm as he slid from the cab. He'd told himself that he needed to get rid of the paintings to keep Samantha from stumbling upon them by accident, but that was only partly true. He couldn't bear to look at the grotesque image of the woman in David's painting another day. At first he'd stared at it for hours, wondering if the abstract portrait was supposed to be Samantha or if it was just a figment of David's imagination. He still wasn't certain. But he was certain that he wanted it out of the house.

He glanced at his watch, mentally calculating how long he'd been gone. Thirty minutes. Today was a milestone for David. He'd been home for five weeks. Daniel smiled. It had taken him every minute of that time to believe that his brother could function on his own. At least during daylight hours. During the day David was safe—sleeping or content just to be in the house. He wouldn't go outside during the day. It was an odd reassurance, but a simple fact.

A bell jangled as Daniel opened the door to the antique shop. "Mose, you in here?"

"Daniel?" The older man's voice called from the storage room. "I'm in the back."

Daniel found Moses bent over an old appliance box, sorting through what looked to him like a tangled heap of junk.

"What a mess."

Moses straightened and smiled as Daniel entered. "Ah . . . only at first glance. Old Miss Tinsdale passed away, and her son-in-law brought by some of her—"

Moses stopped, his gaze fixed on the blanket that covered the paintings. Daniel clutched the canvases tighter, suddenly unsure if he wanted his friend to see David's work, not to mention his own efforts after years without practice. His work was imperfect, but David's was disturbing. And somehow that seemed like another admission of failure where his brother was concerned.

"I have a favor to ask."

Moses's eyes were lit with a brightness Daniel hadn't seen in years. "Tell me you've been painting again and I'll do anything."

"Good, because now that I think about it, I have two favors to ask."

Moses slid his glasses from his nose and tucked them into his shirt pocket. "You haven't told me yet."

"Yes." Daniel hesitated, then set the canvases down, tucking the blanket securely around the edges. "I've been painting, but only to calm David. It seemed important to him that we paint again."

Moses's face broke into a smile. "Hallelujah," he said softly.

"I was hoping you wouldn't mind storing them for me."

Moses waved his hand over the cluttered, dusty storage room. "Pick yourself a corner. What was the second favor?"

"I was wondering if you could stay with David tonight, just long enough to let me get some sleep. I've got an appointment with David's doctor in the morning."

He paused, wondering how much he should tell Moses. The appointment had been made for weeks, but the closer it neared, the more anxious he'd become. The meeting might yield nothing, just another discussion regarding the hopelessness of David's case. Lord knows his mother had been happy to repeat each gloomy report to him over the years. But then again, it might be productive. David's last doctor had finally retired, and a new one had been assigned to his case. And this time Daniel wasn't about to stop until he was certain there was nothing more he could do for his brother.

From outside a siren wailed, and Daniel moved toward the window. The thin glass panes of the old building had long ago been covered with gray paint, but he found a chip in the surface and peered out. A sheriff's car headed south on Main Street, easing its way past shoppers and townspeople as fast as it dared. He caught a glimpse of Francis Smitherman's profile just before the car turned down a side street, its lights flashing as if to herald his self-importance.

Daniel shook his head. He'd known Francis since they were both eight years old. Back then Francis had been a sweaty little kid with a buzz cut. And frankly, Daniel preferred to remember him that way. Before the betrayal. His mind flashed to another time, a time when he'd thought himself in love with Emma. He'd needed her after the fire. Hell, he'd needed anybody. But she'd turned away from him. Instead, she'd turned to Francis.

"My God—" Moses's voice broke.

Daniel turned to find Moses kneeling down next to the paintings, the blanket clutched against his chest. David's painting seemed even more horrific in the cluttered storage room, the woman staring vacantly in Moses's direction.

Moses stood, his eyes moist with emotion as he met Daniel's gaze. "My God, son, what have you done?"

The look on Emma's face made Samantha question her sanity. Why had she felt it necessary to tell Emma about DiCarlo? Why not just make an excuse and terminate their working agreement? Emma wasn't due in to work until Wednesday, and Samantha had worried all week, struggling with how much she needed to tell her. She'd finally decided the sooner the better. Now, faced with the shocked look in her new employee's eyes, she couldn't help but wonder if she'd made the wrong choice.

Samantha felt the heat of tension radiating through her. She'd thought to completely bury her secrets in Scottsdale, but that hadn't happened. Far from it, in fact. Daniel, and now Emma, knew why she was there. She'd decided it was only fair to be honest with Emma about DiCarlo, the trial, and the death threats. But the one thing she hadn't told Emma was that the death threats had followed her to Scottsdale. For some reason she'd needed to hold on to that last piece of information.

One less secret shared. One less vulnerability.

Samantha smoothed a stray strand of hair from her forehead, irritated to find that moisture had beaded there, betraying her own fears. "I'll certainly understand if you don't want to continue working with me."

Emma pulled off the headset to the Dictaphone, which had rested loosely against her shoulders as Samantha explained about the trial. She gestured toward the computer screen. "What about your book?"

Did Emma think the book was a ruse? Of course Samantha knew that wasn't the case, but she couldn't exactly deny that DiCarlo could force her to be deceptive. She felt suddenly embarrassed that she'd brought someone else into the mess her life had become.

"I *am* writing a book on handwriting evaluation and document verification." She tried to make her words even as she spoke. "The writing is temporary, though. When the trial is over I intend to get my business back in full swing—"

"That's not what I meant. I meant who would help you with your book if I quit?"

"I—I don't know. I suppose it would get done eventually."

Emma took a long sip from her coffee mug before she looked up. "Stop looking so worried. I'm not going anywhere."

Samantha breathed a sigh of relief, not because she couldn't manage without help, but because she wanted—needed—some normalcy to remain in her life. "Thank you, but please don't feel obligated—"

Emma waved her hand to silence Samantha. "Enough of that." She pulled her thick curls to one side of her neck and absently massaged her shoulder with her free hand. "Do you think you're safe here?"

Emma's words stopped her short. Was she safe there? No, of course she wasn't. Dante DiCarlo had proved, without a doubt, that she could be found no matter where she hid. He'd changed the rules of his little game, however. The telephone number of where the most recent fax originated had been concealed, listing a series of zeros instead of an actual number. The other faxed threats had intentionally, even proudly, she thought, listed the originating numbers.

Was she supposed to guess where the last message had come from? Was the purpose to make her wonder how closely she was being watched? Samantha glanced around her. She had to admit that the peace she'd first felt at the mansion vanished the night she received the fax.

As she met Emma's expectant gaze, her first instinct was to blurt out the truth, to confess that DiCarlo had found her. But she didn't. "I honestly don't know."

She watched the play of emotion on Emma's face and wondered at her own split-second decision not to tell her the whole truth.

"Ironic." Emma chuckled before her expression altered to one of calm acceptance.

"Why is that?"

"It's just ironic that you chose to come here. To stay here." Emma glanced around as if seeing something that only her eyes could envision. "After all the tragedy this house has seen."

She heard Emma's words, but they didn't make sense. Tragedy? The image of Daniel's face flashed in her mind. He was strong, solid. A shoulder to lean on. Yet there was something innately different about him. His strength carried a certain weariness with it, an intangible sadness.

"You don't know, do you?"

Samantha looked at Emma. The other woman's hand was clamped over her mouth as if she regretted what she'd said, yet her eyes held an odd satisfaction. She shook off the feeling of disappointment. Scottsdale was a small town. Emma was probably just eager to share some gossip.

"No. I don't know what you're talking about." She knew that Emma expected her to ask questions, but the thought of prying into Daniel's past repulsed her.

"Daniel's family died here."

Samantha was certain her face registered shock, but Emma continued as cheerfully as if she were discussing the weather. "There was a house fire."

Samantha glanced around her, as if seeing the apartment for the first time. "How terrible . . ."

"Mm. It happened a long time ago." Emma stood. "Come with me."

"Why?" Samantha followed Emma in a daze. "What—"

"I can't believe he rented you this place without telling you." Emma crossed the small living room and jerked open the apartment door to the foyer. "That's downright mean."

Before Samantha could protest, Emma crossed the foyer and headed toward the interior door that led to the west wing. She vaguely recalled Daniel saying the other wing had been closed off for some time. A waft of cool air drifted over them as Emma opened the door, and chill bumps lifted on Samantha's arms. Had Daniel's family died in this part of the house? Had the damage that he was working to repair been caused by a fire?

"Do you believe in ghosts?"

She looked at Emma in horror. Was she joking? Before Samantha could form a response, Emma disappeared through the doorway.

"Well, well . . ." Emma's voice echoed back to her.

"You shouldn't—" Samantha stopped speaking as she entered the room. What had she expected? Charred remains? A tangible sense of foreboding and death? The room held none of those things.

While her apartment was tidy and functional, the west wing of the house had been restored to what must have been its original appearance. Arched molding over the windows had been painted stark white, and the fresh oil paint reflected the late-afternoon sun that slanted through the windows. Though the flooring showed signs of carpet having been stripped off it, the walls were painted a cheerful creamy yellow.

Samantha was drawn toward the fireplace. A pile of rags and paint stripper rested next to the brick hearth. Daniel must be in the process of stripping the caked layers of old paint from the mantel, she thought. The original bare wood was exposed on one side, revealing an intricately carved design. She smiled. It would be glorious when it was finished.

Outside, the wind whipped the canopy of oak branches, casting a kaleidoscope of dappled sun shadows against the walls. She could envision hardwood floors, classic furniture in shades of pale cream and deep marigold filling the room, the oil painting of the Caldwell mansion hanging over the fireplace. . . .

With a start she realized the path her thoughts had taken. She was acting as if this were *her* house. She glanced at Emma, who was watching her with a curious expression. A deep scowl marred the other woman's face, and the unusual set to her features reminded Samantha that, in fact, she hardly knew Emma Weathers.

"It's so beautiful that it's hard to imagine," Samantha whispered, "that anything tragic ever took place here."

She turned around, taking in the dentil-work crown molding that accented the high ceilings. The room was empty except for a telephone and phone book propped in one corner and a few paint cans and scattered newspapers. But she could envision the room filled with the laughter of family and friends, the homey smell of coffee and homemade bread drifting from the kitchen.

But was she envisioning how the house had once been or how it could be? She decided not to examine her own feelings right then, and instead marveled that Daniel could turn what must have been the most horrible memory of his life into something that welcomed new life, new beginnings.

At that moment she had the distinct feeling that there wasn't anything Daniel Caldwell couldn't do. And despite herself, she wanted to know more about him, his past. In fact, she wanted to know everything there was to know about Daniel.

She looked at Emma, hoping she would continue without being asked. Samantha got her wish.

"Well, something terrible did happen here." Emma cleared her throat and turned her back to Samantha. "No amount of paint can cover that." She sniffed and walked to the window. "The fire didn't take down the whole house, but they died here, or at least Daniel's father did. He died in his sleep."

Samantha felt sick to her stomach. They shouldn't be there, and Emma shouldn't be discussing Daniel's pain so matter-of-factly. Maybe his family's tragedy had become a well-known, well-repeated story in Scottsdale, but the reality of what had happened made her want to clamp her hands over her ears.

Still, something elemental made her need to know more. "Who?" she asked. "Who did he lose in the fire?"

When Emma turned to her, she noticed the other woman's right hand was balled tightly into a fist. Samantha was almost relieved to realize Emma wasn't as hard-hearted as she had sounded.

"The mother lived." Emma's voice echoed harshly against the walls of the empty room.

"Oh," was all Samantha managed.

"But his father died that night from smoke inhalation. He was a drunk. Rumor has it he was too drunk that night to escape the fire."

Again Samantha felt physically sick at Emma's brutal assessment of what had happened. All she could think of was Daniel, his pain. Suddenly she wanted Emma to stop. "I—"

"His little brother died a few days later in the hospital." Emma paused. "But the boy wasn't right to start with."

"So that makes it okay?" Daniel's voice cut through the room like a knife.

Samantha started. "Daniel . . ."

Emma's head snapped around, and she broke into a sincere smile. "I was just giving Samantha the two-dollar tour," she said cheerfully. She crossed the room and laid her hand on his arm. "You know it's been years since I was in this part of the house." She patted his arm as she squeezed past him and into the foyer. "You've worked wonders with it."

Emma leaned back through the doorway and glanced at her watch. "Samantha, I'd better go get the kids. Gus can only stand them underfoot in the store for so long."

Samantha nodded.

Emma gave the room one last appreciative glance and clicked her tongue. "Really, Daniel, you're a miracle worker."

Samantha thought she saw Daniel stiffen, but when he turned to look at Emma his smile was charming. "Good to see you again, Emma."

Samantha stood as if rooted to the floor. What had just happened? For a moment she'd been certain that Daniel and Emma were about to have words. No, more than that. She had gotten the distinct feeling that they were enemies. But she recalled how Emma had pressed her hand against Daniel's arm, and Samantha felt a surge of jealousy. Maybe the tension hadn't been animosity at all.

"Daniel, I'm sorry." She ran her hand through her hair. "We shouldn't have come in here. We—I—had no right."

Daniel caught her arm as she started to move past him. "You had every right to be curious about the rest of the house." He leaned closer, casting a furious glance over his shoulder as the sound of Emma's car engine revving invaded the room. "*You* live here. Emma had no right to try to unnerve you. For the life of me, I don't see why she—"

Samantha laid her free hand on top of his. "I'm sorry."

"It's okay. You aren't to blame."

"No." She met his gaze and watched in amazement as the look in his eyes softened, turning them to a sultry, smoldering green. She swallowed hard. "I meant I was sorry for what happened here."

"It was a long time ago." His voice sounded aloof, but his eyes were fixed on her hand resting atop his. "I survived."

"Thank God," she whispered.

Daniel turned her into his arms and cupped the side of her face with his hand. His eyes narrowed as if he was trying to understand something that puzzled him. "You're not angry with me anymore?"

Her pulse was beating so rapidly, she actually felt light-headed. It took a moment for the meaning of his words to sink in. "The other night I was just . . ." She paused, wondering what she could say.

They'd managed to exchange brief, polite words since the night she'd received the fax. But now she was in his arms again, and there was no denying that she still wanted what she'd wanted from Daniel that night—to make love to him.

What would he do if she told him that she still wanted him? She'd reached out to him once, laid her heart and her feelings on the line. No, she wouldn't give in so easily to temptation this time. This time she would wait for him.

"You were right." She cleared her throat. "I was frightened."

Daniel dropped his hand and nodded.

Her heart felt heavy, and a sudden panic gripped her. Right then and there she knew it. She would wait for Daniel if it took the rest of her life.

Samantha watched the shadows dance on the ceiling. Sleep hadn't come easily since the death threats started, but somehow the worry felt different that night. She couldn't put her finger on it, but something was wrong. It nibbled at the edge of her awareness but never came to the forefront of her mind.

Emma's behavior that afternoon had been bizarre and out of character, to say the least. She closed her eyes, and her thoughts instantly turned to Daniel. He'd looked at her with something more than sympathy or mild interest. Samantha hugged her arms against her chest and smiled. If someone had asked her about falling in love a month ago, she would have said she'd never done it. And that was true. But what she wouldn't have known was how little she understood love.

And now that it was happening to her, it was the most exhilarating, frightening feeling she'd ever known.

She threw the heavy comforter back and sat up. This was ridiculous. She couldn't sleep but she could at least work. Nightfall had lowered the temperature in the old house, and she slid her arms into her thin cotton housecoat and tied the sash tightly around her waist. But when she plopped down into her office chair she knew concentration was out of the question. The fax machine, though once again unplugged, stared at her like a silent reminder of the danger that remained.

Pace. That's what she'd always done when the right word wouldn't come to her for a client's report, or when the books didn't balance. Or, she realized, when the loneliness had become too hard to bear. She hadn't noticed the small apartment contained so much furniture until her third pass through the living room and another bruise on her shins. Before she knew what she was doing, she found herself standing in the empty foyer, facing the door that led to the west wing.

You can't go in there, her conscience whispered. But she didn't listen. Something was drawing her to that room as surely as she was drawn to Daniel. She almost expected to find him waiting for her on the other side, but she was met with a bone-chilling emptiness instead.

Samantha found the wall switch and was relieved when the overhead fixture came to life. Then she saw it—the solitary telephone in the corner. She stopped, her thoughts jumbled. Daniel didn't have phone service to the guest house but he had gone to the trouble of installing a phone in this part of the house? Why? It didn't make sense. She picked her way barefoot across the gritty floor, avoiding discarded nails and splintered wood. Kneeling next to the telephone, she lifted the receiver.

The gentle hum of the dial tone answered the question in her mind. On impulse she slid the phone directory out from under the phone. A paint stick marked a place in the yellow business section. When she allowed the pages to fall open, she felt her heart sink. "Facsimiles, fax service, fax machines," the heading read. The phone book hit the floor with a dull thud.

Now she knew what had been circling in her mind all night, what had been out of place. She arranged the phone book and telephone at exactly the angle she had found them and stood. Chill bumps raised on her arms as the quiet cold of the empty room found her beneath her thin housecoat.

Was it possible that someone could have sent the last fax from this very room? She stood motionless in the vacant room and closed her eyes.

This time when she willed the emptiness to return, it obeyed.

SEVEN

The faint odor of smoke wasn't unpleasant, just annoying. Samantha rolled to her side and pulled the bedspread over her bare shoulders. Pressing her face against the pillowcase she inhaled the fragrance of the clean fabric. Still the odor of smoke found her again. She slowly opened her eyes.

Fire.

She bolted upright, confused. A quick glance told her that the room wasn't on fire. But the smell?

When her gaze fell on the window, she understood. A deep red glow came from the thicket of woods that lined the back side of the estate, outlining the guest cottage like a photo negative. Her instincts told her the fire was moving toward the two houses, but her heart could hold only one thought: Daniel.

She threw the covers from the bed and swung her feet to the floor. *Think, Samantha.* Clothes. She needed clothes. The thin nightgown was discarded and instantly replaced by the first thing she encountered in her closet—blue jeans and a cotton sweater. She'd just pulled on socks and tennis shoes when someone began pounding on the door.

"Samantha! Samantha, open up." Daniel's voice was commanding, even through the door that separated them.

She opened the door just as he was about to pound on it a second time. His gaze raked her from head to toe, the expression on his face registering surprise.

"Good. You're awake." He combed his hand through his hair and glanced anxiously over his shoulder. "There's a woods fire. I wanted to make sure you were up in case we don't get it under control. I'll check on you when I get back."

She joined him in the foyer and closed the door behind her. "I'm going too."

She was what? Daniel stared down at the determined look on her face. "That's not necessary. The volunteer fire department is on their way."

Samantha pulled her hair into a ponytail and secured it with a band. "Well, they just got another volunteer."

He looked away, unable to meet her gaze any longer. The first thought he'd had when realizing the woods were on fire had been Samantha. He felt a familiar pang of guilt. Moses was with David, and he'd given them instructions to leave if the fire jumped the woods, but she'd been the first thought that entered his mind. Lord, what was happening to him?

He knew the answer as soon as the question formed

in his mind. He was falling in love with Samantha Delaney. The realization almost made him laugh with relief. He'd walled himself away like a monk for almost
half his life, afraid to reach out to anyone in Scottsdale,
afraid of the scorn. Yet he'd been even more leery of
finding someone who would tempt him to leave behind
his responsibilities.

Yet he'd fallen for Samantha. With her own ready-
made problems and literally surrounded by danger, she
was the last person he should fall in love with. But it
was too late. Honor had kept him from making love to
her when she'd asked, yet the pain of denial had been
more than physical. *Denial.* How long had it been since
he'd actually felt strongly enough about something—
much less someone—to feel denied?

He took a deep breath. "Look, I just wanted to
make sure you knew where I was and what was going
on. The fire isn't that involved yet. Go back to bed."

"It's not an emergency?"

"That depends on your definition of emergency."
She continued to stare at him, and he shook his head.
"Not yet."

Her expression a curious mix of anger and sadness,
she said, "In that case, follow me."

He followed her across the foyer and was surprised
when she approached the door to the west wing. She
opened it and entered without hesitation, the soft soles
of her tennis shoes whispering across the floor until she
stopped at the fireplace.

"Explain this," she stated, her voice a monotone.
She knelt down and retrieved the phone book he'd left

in the corner, then turned to face him. She gestured to the phone that sat there. "You have phone service in an unused portion of this house but none in your own?"

Daniel glanced down at the telephone. The technician had just finished installing the service, both to the guest cottage and the west wing. But what difference did that make? And why, for God's sake, did Samantha look as if she were accusing him of something?

"Yesterday." He propped his hands against his hips and examined her face in the near darkness. "They hooked the service up yesterday . . . here and in the guest cottage." He closed the distance between them, never letting his gaze fall from hers. Stopping inches from her, he cocked his head and watched her nerve falter. "Why do you ask?"

Her fingers curled around a paint-encrusted wooden stick that was stuck between the pages of the phone book. She slipped her fingers into the crevice and allowed the phone book to fall open. He recognized the section of the yellow pages immediately, but not the section she pointed to.

"Now explain this." Her voice was a mere whisper but raspy with tension.

Daniel struggled to read the words in the half-light of the room. "Fax machines?" Realization hit him before his voice finished echoing off the walls of the room.

Samantha only stared up at him, the fear and trepidation in her eyes speaking for her.

"You—" He grabbed her by the shoulders and

stopped just short of shaking her. "You think I sent that fax?"

"I—I don't know." Her face was pale but she didn't pull away. Instead she stared at him. Waiting.

"Why on God's earth would I do that?"

"DiCarlo . . ." She looked ill as she spoke his name. "He only needs to frighten me away, to convince me not to testify. He—he could offer you anything."

"And I have nothing." Daniel heard the cynicism in his own voice. "Is that right?"

"No." Her eyes were round with emotion as she shook her head. "I never meant that."

He pulled the phone book from her hand and jabbed his finger at another heading. "Fireplace." He watched the dawning cross her face but couldn't take pleasure in it. She'd accused him. She'd thought . . . He jabbed at the heading a second time, his anger mounting. "Fireplace, Samantha. I need someone to clean the chimney. It hasn't been used in years."

She glanced over her shoulder but didn't respond. He could see the emotional battle playing across her face. She believed him. He instinctively knew that. But she wasn't about to apologize for protecting herself. And, he realized, she shouldn't have to.

He threw the phone book onto the floor, the loud slapping sound breaking the silence. Reaching out, he ran the tip of his finger across her jawline. She shivered beneath his touch. He slowly tilted her face to meet his. "You're not alone anymore, Samantha." He shook his head as she started to protest. "You can trust me."

She nodded.

From outside came the muted sound of men's voices and the wail of sirens. He dropped his hand and willed himself to step away from her, to completely break the spell. "I've got a fire to fight."

This time she smiled. "We've got a fire to fight."

He looped his arm around her shoulders, a silent truce. "Maybe the firefighters could use another hand."

It was true that it would take the efforts of neighbors as well as the volunteer firefighters to put the fire out. The routine of fighting brush fires was, unfortunately, well-known to the townspeople of Scottsdale. He couldn't recall a single fall season when a woods fire didn't threaten someone's home or land. Daniel looked at the determined set to Samantha's mouth and nodded. If she was going to help fight the fire, she was going to do it where she'd be safe—right beside him.

When they stepped out of the house, their path was lit by the ominous glow of the fire. Emergency vehicles had pulled into the courtyard that separated the mansion from the guest house, and neighbors had begun to follow suit. Teenage boys and elderly men, housewives and shop owners, they piled from their vehicles.

Samantha cupped her hands together to be heard over the commotion. "How bad is it?"

"It looks bad, but it isn't," Daniel answered. "There's a relatively small area of woods—about five acres or so—before you reach a road that runs parallel to Main Street. The road is a natural break and so is the lawn here. Besides, there isn't enough land back there for it to get too big."

"How did it start?" she asked, her voice distractingly breathless and sultry as they walked toward the scene.

Daniel felt the smoke stinging his lungs as they neared the fire. He shook his head. "I'm not sure. There's an elderly man named Mr. Dennis who lives about a half mile from here. He was burning leaves earlier today but swears the fire was out."

He left it at that. What he didn't say was that he believed Mr. Dennis, and that from what he saw, the fire had originated in more than one spot. He grimaced as a small pine tree burst into flames in the distance, shooting soot and sparks into the night sky. One well-placed spark against the old wooden structure of either house, and it could spell disaster.

He stared at the guest cottage, now only yards from them. Moses could be trusted to keep David safe, but he honestly didn't know how his brother would react— how he might deal with the memories—if he realized the fire was creeping up the hill behind the house. Was he doing the right thing by leaving them alone? His instincts told him that Samantha could be trusted with his secret about David if need be, but he couldn't imagine such a crash course in reality, under the circumstances.

"Should we start wetting down the yard and courtyard?" Samantha stopped and glanced around her. "Or do you think we would be of more help going in the back?"

He couldn't help but smile. "Now what does a city girl like you know about fighting fires?"

She laughed, and the sound almost made him forget the chaos that was going on around them. "Enough to know I need a pair of gloves and a rake or a shovel. Besides, I wasn't always a city girl."

"In here." He pressed his hand against her back and guided her toward the storage shed.

In a few seconds they emerged with gloves, a shovel, and an old broom. Samantha quirked one eyebrow when he handed her the broom.

"Save that comment." He threw up his hands. "The broom is lighter and it'll actually do more good than anything else."

"Fine." Samantha smiled as she tugged the broom from Daniel's grip, allowing her gaze to linger on his face a little longer than necessary. How could she have possibly doubted him? She'd seen the wounded look in his eyes when she showed him the phone book, though it had lasted for only a moment. In the next moment he'd been concerned with her, asking for her trust, reassuring her.

He turned and started toward the burning woods at a near jog, and she followed. She grew apprehensive, though, as they approached the fire. She'd barely noticed the lay of the land behind the guest cottage, had never ventured farther than the courtyard, but it had appeared to be a dense area of hardwood and pine tangled with a thick growth of underbrush. Now the underbrush had either burned away or was on fire, and the newly cleared area at the base of the trees was a carpet of glowing embers.

"Where do you want me?"

"With me."

Samantha felt her heart leap at the husky, possessive sound of his voice. She tried to shake the feeling. He was, after all, referring to the best way to tackle the fire. But when she glanced at his face, she wasn't so sure. Something in Daniel's eyes was different that night, and it had nothing to do with the crisis they faced. There was a confidence, a determination that was directed solely at her.

She slid the gloves on and tried to concentrate on the situation facing them. "Let's go."

"This way." Daniel headed toward the line of burning trees and underbrush.

Samantha glanced at the sparks soaring through the sky. Most of them cooled in the moist night air, losing their glow long before they fell. But a few did make it back to the ground, still glowing with life and ready to ignite anything they came in contact with.

"What about the houses?" she asked.

Even from behind him, she could see Daniel stiffen. As if in answer to her question, he pulled one of the firefighters aside. He had to shout to be heard above the crackling of the fire and the voices of the other volunteers. "It shouldn't take much work to keep the blaze away from the lawn," he told the man, "but keep an eye on the houses. Watch the roofs for debris."

Daniel spoke to the firefighter as if he were his superior. Samantha cringed, fully expecting the other man to take offense. Instead he glanced toward the guest cottage and the mansion with determination. "We won't let anything happen to them."

"Is anyone going to work the fire line on the east side?" Daniel gestured toward the woods. "The Coopers' house isn't that far. It might be in danger."

The fireman paused. "Yeah, I've got enough people to keep it under control up here. But on the lower half of that slope . . ." He shook his head. "I don't know about that."

"Then we'll go down the hill and work the east side."

The other man nodded and clasped Daniel on the shoulder. "Be careful. The winds are shifting, and that incline is treacherous."

Daniel turned to Samantha. "Are you sure?"

She suddenly felt a pang of fear, but when she met his eyes an unexpected calm came over her. "Yes."

They stepped over the low flames that had now found the edge of the courtyard, then skirted the worst of the fire by entering the woods along the edge that was still unharmed by the flames.

Soon they were a safe distance from the fire, giving the glowing fire line a surreal look. There was a certain peace in the cool shelter of the woods, though the shouts and commotion of the volunteers still drifted through the trees. Then, as if to remind them of the danger, the winds shifted, blowing a thick wall of smoke into their faces. It surrounded them, covering them in a blanket of choking ash. Samantha felt herself grow nauseous with the effort it took to breathe. But just as suddenly the wind swirled away again, and the air cleared.

"Are you okay?" Daniel turned to face her.

She nodded and wiped tears from her stinging eyes. "I'm fine."

He flashed a smile that made her believe she looked like something other than a soot-covered orphan. Pushing aside low-growing branches, he resumed their trek through the thick underbrush. "So what did you mean back there?" he asked.

"About what?"

"You said you hadn't always been a city girl."

"Oh." She had already forgotten that she said as much. "I wasn't raised in Atlanta. I spent the early part of my childhood in a small town like Scottsdale."

"How did you end up in the city?" He spoke without slowing, his voice never reflecting the physical exertion it took to maneuver through the thick woods.

"I—we—my father changed jobs." She heard the hesitation in her own voice. "He took a position in Atlanta."

"Why?"

Samantha ground her teeth. Why all the sudden questions from Daniel? They were stomping through the woods in the middle of a forest fire, for heaven's sake. She didn't want to talk about her childhood or her parents. She'd dealt with being alone for the past nine years. Wasn't it enough that she'd survived on her own? She'd never understood the compulsion of others to make her talk about the past.

"It was a better job, more money." She decided to

get the inevitable over with. "He was worried about paying for my education."

Daniel stopped dead in his tracks in front of her. For a moment she thought he intended to continue the ridiculous discussion right there in the middle of nowhere, but to her surprise he took a few steps backward, then jumped a ravine that stretched in front of them.

Samantha stood there like a statue. If Daniel hadn't been in the lead, she would probably have tumbled headfirst into the narrow but deep gully. The glow from the fire was enough to light their way, but the rocky ravine looked as innocent as the forest floor until you were right on it.

"So, do your parents still live in Atlanta?" Daniel pushed back fallen leaves until the opposite edge of the ravine was fully visible.

He expected her to jump. But in her mind she didn't see the ravine, the fire, or even Daniel. In her mind she saw the look on her teacher's face as she was handed a note. *Samantha, would you mind stepping outside the classroom?* The teacher's voice had trembled and she had cried when she delivered the news. *Your parents have been in a terrible accident. . . .* But the woman's sympathy had been useless.

Grieving was useless. Nothing could bring her parents back, return to her the love she'd known and lost. Nothing could ease the pain. Nothing except the emptiness.

"Samantha?" Daniel's voice penetrated her thoughts.

She looked up just in time to receive a hot gust of smoke directly in her face. Following Daniel's gaze, she saw that the fire line was moving with the wind. Toward them.

She realized, then, what the questions had been about. A distraction. The fire line had slowly been traveling in their direction. She'd thought they were moving toward it, but it was the other way around.

"Take my hand." Daniel leaned over the ravine. "I won't let you fall."

I'm sorry, Samantha, but your parents didn't survive the accident.

"They're dead." She shouted the words over the sound of the hungry fire. To her left a fallen pine tree blazed with life. She watched through tears as a look of total confusion came over Daniel's face. "My parents"—she paused, forcing her voice to stop trembling—"died in a car accident when I was eighteen."

He glanced at the growing flames, then back at her. "You need to jump, Samantha. The clearing is just ahead." He pulled off his gloves and inched his hand a little closer. "You can trust me."

She smiled, ignoring the fresh dusting of hot ashes that prickled the skin of her face and hands, and pulled off her own gloves. She reached for Daniel's hand. Their fingers barely touched until she leaped over the ravine, but before her feet even touched the ground her hand was caught firmly in Daniel's and she was in his arms.

He held her that way, amid the danger of fire and the unrelenting winds, for what seemed like an eternity. When her knees shook, he held her up. When the sobs wouldn't subside, he whispered sweet words of comfort against her hair. With each tear the emptiness left, opening a part of her that had been sealed away by bitterness and pain. Samantha wrapped her arms tighter around Daniel's shoulders and let the emptiness drift away. Little by little it left her, and little by little she was filled up again. By Daniel, by strength and love.

By the time the winds shifted away again, she'd stopped crying. She threw her head back and stared up into the night sky. The stars were covered, the moon concealed by smoke and ash, but still she felt it. Freedom. The same wind that carried the danger dried her tears. A half sob, half laugh escaped her, sounding strangely at home in the wilderness that surrounded them. She looked into Daniel's face and met his gaze, filled with tenderness and understanding. The future.

He cupped her face in his hands and leaned forward until his breath was against her ear. "I knew you could do it," he whispered.

Tears threatened to spill again, and she bit her lip. "I didn't."

He brushed his lips against hers, then straightened to look over her shoulder, a worried frown creasing his brow. "We've got to go."

She stepped back and tugged her gloves into place, a new energy filling her, pushing her into motion. The danger existed, the fire steadily moved toward them, but it no longer mattered. Not only would she survive, from now on she would live.

She waited while Daniel pulled on his own gloves, then, just as naturally, entwined his fingers with hers. But this time when they headed into the thicket, Daniel didn't let go.

"Damn." The single word was absorbed by the shifting smoke. It had been easy enough to go unnoticed in the confusion, but it would be impossible to jump that ravine without being heard. Another missed opportunity. And another touching scene. Hatred bubbled up like an acid burn that would likely last until dawn.

Samantha and Daniel moved farther into the woods, hand in hand, finally disappearing behind the veil of smoke. Ah, how easy it would have been for an unexpected wall of fire to trap them. The can of kerosene was lowered into a leaf-covered hole, a convenient hiding place left, by chance, by a rotted pine tree. Perfect. Yes, opportunity had a way of presenting itself. Again and again. Over and over.

Until it was done.

Three hours of the most backbreaking work she'd ever experienced and Samantha was ready to drop. The broom, which was now no more than a comical-looking stump, trailed behind her as she dragged it through the soot and dying embers. She could feel the heat of the earth penetrating her tennis shoes, and knew there probably wasn't much left of the thin rubber soles.

She and Daniel had made it safely to the rear of the fire and had secured the east side, eventually battling their way back toward the mansion. They'd worked side by side most of the time, Daniel seeking her out and pulling her back next to him if she ever strayed. But something else had happened during the night. She smiled and looked at her gloved hand resting solidly in Daniel's.

One by one, Daniel stopped to shake the hands of his neighbors with reserved gratitude. But, she realized with a pang of excitement, he never released hers. They watched neighbors and volunteers drifting toward their vehicles and loading up equipment. The crisis might be over, but something else had begun. Something between them.

"What time is it?" she whispered, her voice raspy from the smoke, as the last fire and rescue truck pulled away.

He dropped her hand just long enough to remove his gloves and step into the circle of a truck's headlights. He checked his watch. "Three o'clock." He met her eyes and tugged her gloves off—first one and then the other. This time when he entwined his fingers with hers, flesh met flesh. "Time to get you back home."

Home. The word sounded natural to her ears. Atlanta had been home for the past nine years, but it had never actually felt like home. Suddenly Scottsdale did. Maybe it was the fact that the glorious old mansion had survived another crisis, or maybe it was the pulling together of the community. She wasn't sure. She had an idea, though, that it was none of those things. It was Daniel.

"Wait here," he whispered as they reached the guest cottage. He took the stairs two at a time and disappeared through the door.

For an instant she thought she heard voices, but just as quickly Daniel reappeared. He didn't say anything, simply drew her hand back into his and headed for the mansion.

"Is everything okay?" she asked.

He nodded and crossed the dark courtyard in silence, tugging her behind him as fast as her weary legs would go. When they took the unlighted porch stairs at breakneck speed, she planted her feet firmly at the top and refused to budge. "Daniel—what's wrong?"

"Nothing." It was difficult to distinguish details in the darkness, but she saw that his eyes were lit with an almost manic energy. She glanced at the porch light, surprised to see that it wasn't on. But when he wrapped his hand around her arm and pulled her against the side of the house, all other thoughts were lost.

Daniel's mouth was on hers before she realized he was going to kiss her. Her own mouth opened voluntarily, her hands tangling in his hair, pulling him, urging him to deepen the kiss.

The smoky-sweet smell of the fire clung to their skin and clothes, reminding her of the crisis that had bonded them. Daniel tugged her hair from the band that bound it, and the motion only opened her mouth farther to his kisses. She heard a deep moan rumble in his throat as his tongue dipped and teased within her mouth.

Her body sagged against the hard surface of the house, exposing her hips to Daniel's thrusts, his arousal grinding against her in a sweet promise of what could be.

"Daniel . . ."

He didn't answer, but reached around her to find the door handle. As soon as she heard the heavy door bump against the inner wall, Daniel tugged her inside the foyer. Again she was pressed against a wall, his body and mouth covering hers. Never in her life had she thought such passion was possible—in herself or anyone else.

He grabbed the bottom of her soot-streaked sweater and tugged it upward until it cleared her arms. He flung it on the hardwood floor as if it were offensive for having covered her body. When he turned to her again, he paused. Without a word he found the light switch that illuminated the chandelier above them, bathing them both in a soft yellow glow. In her earlier panic, she hadn't put on a bra, and his eyes registered surprise when he gazed at her naked breasts.

His lips parted, and she thought for a moment that he was going to say something. Instead he dropped to his knees and took one breast fully in his mouth. Samantha felt her knees buckle at the warm, damp feel of his mouth and tongue against the sensitive flesh of her nipple. He trailed kisses across her stomach and popped the brad to her jeans.

"Wait," she whispered.

He ignored her, unzipping the zipper and tugging on the stiff material.

"Daniel, wait."

This time he stood, his body raking against hers as he did. He pulled his shirt off, exposing a wide expanse of slick, muscled chest. "We've waited long enough." His words were raspy against her ear, his desire clear in his voice.

She stared at his chest, then at the tempting curl of dark hair that drew a line from the top of his jeans to the flat muscles of his chest.

"Inside." She kicked off her ruined shoes, tugged off her socks, and started to open the door to her apartment.

Daniel grabbed her arm and looked down at her with an amused grin. "You might as well take everything else off."

She smiled up at him. "Is that so?"

He shook his head, a serious look on his face. "The soot."

"Oh." She pretended to be offended. "If it bothers you, then . . ."

He hooked his thumbs over the waistband of her jeans and pushed them to the floor, taking her panties with them. "Does that answer your question?"

"I think so," she whispered. She stepped out and kicked free of them, suddenly aware that she was standing, fully nude, in front of Daniel.

"You"—his gaze never left hers, but he unsnapped his jeans as he spoke—"are beautiful." He took a step closer to her, and the sound of his zipper punctuated his sentence. His mouth closed over hers and she felt the brush of his jeans as he pushed free of them. Then he was against her, and the readiness of his arousal took her breath away.

"Wait." She fumbled for the apartment door as he pressed his hips against hers, his erection probing impatiently against the soft folds of her thighs.

"Uh-uh." The words were barely discernible as he rubbed his unshaven jaw against her nipples. "No more waiting."

She got the door open, taking him with her as they stumbled into the living room. One of his hands was against her back and the other broke their fall as Daniel pushed them to the thick carpet.

"My God, you take my breath away." He leaned over her, his eyes boring into hers. "I love you, Samantha Delaney," he whispered.

She felt tears form and spill in the instant he spoke. How could she have not known? How could she have needed so desperately to hear those words and not known? She brushed her fingertips against his face. "Then make love to me." She felt the sweet pressure of his erection against her and parted her legs. "No more waiting," she whispered.

He was inside her in the breath of a moment, filling her until she thought she'd cry out from pleasure. He hesitated only a moment before he began moving inside her, each gentle thrust becoming more and more urgent.

"Daniel. . . ." She heard herself speak his name as if she were dreaming.

He slowed and she opened her eyes. His hair was tousled and hanging in his face; the thick muscles of his shoulders were bunched with the effort of his control. Their eyes met and she knew. The joining of their bodies was as right as the joining of their souls.

"I love you," she whispered as she felt the sweet building of her release.

Daniel moaned and thrust within her again, this time without restraint. She felt his release just as she found her own.

Samantha wrapped her wet hair in a towel and eased into bed next to Daniel. She curled against his side, her hand trailing over his chest as if to reassure herself that he was real, that their lovemaking hadn't been only in her imagination. He wrapped his arm around her shoulders, and she nestled her head in the crook of his arm. His skin smelled of soap and warmth, and she inhaled the scent, committing the moment to memory.

Never had she felt such passion. And never had she felt so desired. Daniel had made love to her as if they were in a dream, fulfilling her every need. Yet he was still there—in the flesh—and as real as she was. Now cool and fresh from her shower, she felt more content than she had in ages. A pang of realization hit her. She was as happy as she'd ever been, even before her parents' deaths.

Then she heard it, a soft shuffling followed by a muted thump. At first she thought the sound was one of the many creaks and settling noises of the old house, but there was something too familiar about it. She sat up, thankful for the darkness that still encased the room.

Daniel shifted beside her. "What's wrong?"

She slipped from the bed and tightened the belt of her robe. "Nothing."

He sat up. "Where are you going?"

"Just to get us something to drink. How about a soda?"

"That'd be good." His voice sounded suspicious.

"I'll be right back." She forced herself to seem cheerful, but fear was choking her. Dear God, what if she was right?

Her feet carried her toward her office, but the movement of her own body felt disjointed from her thoughts, from the fear that begged her to stay by Daniel's side and ignore the possibilities. As she walked through the door to the office she saw it. The small green light of the fax machine's power button would seem innocent under any other circumstances, but tonight it started her whole world spinning out of control again. She clasped her hand over her mouth to muffle a scream.

"No," she whispered as she walked toward her desk. She thought of the sheer bliss she'd known just moments ago in Daniel's arms. She shook her head. "This isn't happening. Not tonight. Not now."

Just four steps and she was standing at her desk. Her fingers trembled as she switched on the desk lamp. The warm yellow glow cast its light over the office wall, the polished oak surface of the desk, the flower arrangement she'd bought downtown. She allowed her gaze to travel over all of those things, purposely avoiding the one thing she needed to check. But finally she forced herself to look at the fax machine.

It was there, of course. Waiting for her. She lifted the sheet of paper from the message tray and laid it instantly on the desk, unable to touch it for any length of time. She couldn't ignore the message, though, written in thick bold print. *That was a close one.* The words seemed to jump off the page. She stumbled backward, feeling assaulted by the five words on the paper.

Daniel caught her by the shoulders. She turned to find he'd slipped on his jeans, but his bare chest and damp hair reminded her that they'd just made love. She wanted to step into his arms. She wanted to lean her head against his strong shoulder and disappear. If only all that which threatened her would disappear as easily.

"What is it?" He touched the side of her face and inched her chin up until she met his gaze.

When she couldn't force the words out, he eased her to one side and walked the short distance to her desk. A muttered curse was all he allowed himself before straightening and turning back to her.

"Samantha, it's okay. You've already received one threat. We knew this might happen again."

She shook her head. "No, you don't understand. Close call. . . . He's talking about the fire tonight. He not only knows where I am, he's here too."

Daniel's expression was deadly. "We'll let Francis know right away." He turned and grasped the fax ma-

chine with both hands, and for a moment she thought
he would fling it across the room.

"Daniel"—her words faltered, and the trembling
began—"you don't understand."

He moved to take her in his arms. "Shh. It's going
to be all right." He rocked her back and forth and
planted kisses against the side of her neck. "He may
know that you're in Scottsdale, but he can't get to you
here at the house. You're safe."

"No." She pulled out of his arms and shook her
head. "You don't understand."

"What, then?"

She pointed to her desk. "The fax machine was unplugged when we left."

EIGHT

Daniel stared at Samantha, then at the room she'd made her office. Someone had been there, had invaded her privacy and his home. Had DiCarlo's people known that she was gone when they entered? He felt his shoulder muscles knot with tension at the thought. Either way, he'd be damned if he'd let that happen again.

He snatched up the phone, then hesitated. What was the damned number to the guest house, anyway? He punched out what he hoped was the right sequence of numbers and waited for an answer.

"Hello." Moses's voice sounded tired.

"Hey, it's Daniel."

He heard Moses shuffle, as if sitting upright. "Daniel. Is everything okay?"

"No."

"The fire is under control, isn't it?"

"Yeah." He paused, not knowing how much to say.

"It's Samantha. She's in danger and I'm going to spend the night. Can you stay a little longer?"

"Sure." Moses's voice took on an excited tone.

No doubt the older man thought it was merely a convenient excuse. After all, Daniel had just announced that he was staying the rest of the night with a beautiful woman. He sighed. If only it were that simple.

He decided to let the misconception stand. He didn't want to go into detail over the phone, and he'd rather not rehash the chain of events in front of Samantha. He glanced in her direction and smiled, hoping to reassure her. She returned his smile, though hers was less than confident.

"Thanks," he said to Moses. "You've been saving my life lately."

"Don't worry about it. Everything is fine here." Moses chuckled. "It's almost sunup and David just fell asleep. Darnedest thing, that boy."

"Good. I'll be there as soon as I can."

"What about your appointment with David's doctor?"

"Dammit. It's at one o'clock." He glanced at his wrist to find his watch wasn't there. Then he remembered that he'd thrown it, along with his clothes, on the floor. He'd gone from the heaven of Samantha's arms to the hell of knowing she was in imminent danger. Amazing.

"Don't worry." Moses sounded calm. "You can still make it if you can get a little sleep. I'll cover for you as long as you need me."

"I owe you."

Moses chuckled. "Of course you do, son." Then he hung up the phone.

Daniel stared at the phone for a minute after replacing the receiver. So far Moses had been the only person he felt he could trust with the truth about David. That was about to change. It had to.

He took Samantha by both hands and looked into her eyes. "There's something I need to tell you."

The expression on her face was wary, and she shook her head. "Nothing good ever started with that sentence."

"When you thought you heard someone in your apartment last weekend, you did."

She paled visibly. "DiCarlo."

"No, it was my brother." Daniel watched her expression go from terrified to disbelieving. "David."

"But Emma said that—"

"I know what Emma said, what she thinks." He tried to find the right words, but what could he say that wouldn't frighten her? He took a deep breath. "We allowed everyone—everyone in Scottsdale that knew us—to believe that David had died. But he didn't. He's alive and staying with me in the guest cottage."

She shook her head. "I don't understand. Why?"

Daniel released her hands and shoved his fingers into the top of his jeans pockets. "Something about David is different. I can't explain it. I don't even understand it myself, but it's been that way since he was just a kid. My mother could never accept David because of it."

He ran his hand through his hair. He wanted to be

anywhere, to be doing anything, other than standing in front of Samantha reciting the pain his family had inflicted on one another. But he had to. He recalled the anguish on Samantha's face earlier that night as she'd told him of her parents' deaths. He walked over to the fax machine and jerked the plug from the socket. She'd been through enough.

But at least, it seemed, she and her parents had loved one another. He doubted his family had ever evolved that far. No, that wasn't true. He loved David. And now he loved Samantha.

"There's more, isn't there?"

He turned to face her. The look in her eyes was one of understanding. She laid her hand against his arm, and he felt the acceptance he'd looked for all his life. It was there for him. He prayed it would be there for David.

"My brother is bright and intuitive. He may not be like other kids—other men—but I'll swear . . ." He shook his head, knowing the full truth was inevitable. "David was blamed for the fire that killed my father."

"Oh, Daniel." She clasped her hands over her mouth but didn't move. In fact, she looked as if she wanted to bolt from the room.

Who could blame her if she did? Hadn't she gone through enough with DiCarlo already? He knew his next words could easily break her composure.

"My mother sent David to a full-care facility thirteen years ago." He paused, watching Samantha's face. "For the mentally ill. She passed away last year, and I've been hacking my way through red tape, trying to get him home, ever since. He's been home for a little more than a month now."

She remained calm, standing motionless for a moment, then she turned and walked from the room. Dammit, what had he expected? He gave her a minute, then followed the path she'd taken to the kitchen. When he caught up with her, she was leaning against the counter, staring out the window toward the guest house.

Daniel stopped a few feet away, barely resisting the urge to reach for her. He could read the tension in the taut lines of her back and shoulders beneath her sheer robe. She didn't need another complication; she was going through hell in her own life right now.

But David was his brother, a part of him. His responsibility. Period.

And yet he loved Samantha. In the short time he'd known her, she'd given him hope for the future. Hell, she was his future as far as he was concerned. The truth was, he wasn't willing to give up either of them.

"What are you thinking?" he asked when she didn't acknowledge his presence.

She didn't turn to face him, only chuckled softly. "That I'll trade you one crazed organized crime boss for your brother."

She was making a joke? He'd deceived her, possibly endangered her life, and she was able to laugh about it? He felt the tension within him uncoil and shook his head in disbelief. She was a rare find.

He decided to test her sense of humor. "Throw in one phantom black Labrador and it's a deal."

This time she whirled to face him, her gaze piercing and not a humorous expression in sight. "What are you talking about?"

Uh-oh, he thought, too much too soon. He had the feeling Samantha's understanding nature was about to be pushed past the limit of endurance. He balled his fists to resist the urge to take her into his arms. When he held her, everything fell into place, everything was—

"What, Daniel?" She took a step toward him, her gaze suspicious. "Tell me now."

"You never hit a black dog like the sheriff insisted you did. It was David." His voice was low, the shame of his deceit evident even in his voice.

"I—I hit your brother?" Her eyes widened with horror. "Oh my God . . ."

"No." He grabbed her shoulders and forced her to look at him. "You ran over his backpack." Then Daniel recalled the way David had announced, in his blasé manner, that he needed a new backpack. He stifled the urge to laugh. Judging from the look in her eyes, Samantha would beat him to a bloody pulp if he started laughing now. But he felt the corners of his mouth twitch despite himself.

"This is funny?" She pulled free and came at him, her right hand curled into a tight little fist, and hit him square on the arm. Then she stopped, a look of relief replacing the anger. "I knew it. I knew it wasn't a dog." Her voice rose. "Why would the sheriff insist he saw a dead dog?"

Daniel shrugged. "Maybe he was trying to reassure you."

"Or humor me," she said softly. She looked away for a moment, and when she met his gaze again he saw the anger was back. "And you—why didn't you tell me? Daniel, I've been sick with worry thinking that I'd hurt someone."

"I'm sorry." He held out both hands, praying she would respond. "David's coming home is complicated. I don't want anyone to know he's here until he's had a chance to settle in."

To his relief Samantha not only slid her hands into his, but stepped into his embrace. Daniel felt his world was right again as he wrapped his arms around her, and nuzzled the exposed skin on her neck.

He'd found the other half of himself, of his soul. And the thought of losing her was unbearable.

She nuzzled the side of his neck. "The phone call. . . . Do you need to go home?"

He recognized the exhaustion in her voice and hugged her tighter. "No. A friend is staying with David tonight. There's no way I'm leaving you."

She sighed. "When can I meet him?"

Daniel was grateful that she couldn't see the shocked expression on his face. Until that moment it hadn't occurred to him that she would want to meet David. "Uh . . . soon, I hope. I'll let you know when I think he's ready."

"Okay." Her voice was a mere whisper, and she leaned heavily against him.

The physical and emotional demands of the last

several hours had finally taken their toll, he realized. He pointed her toward the bedroom. "You need some rest."

"No argument here," she said as she headed toward the hallway.

"I'll be right there," he called after her.

When he made a quick check of the front door, he found it unlocked. He barely resisted the urge to punch the wall. They'd fallen through the door with nothing on their minds except making love. He stiffened as he recalled how easily the door had opened. Samantha hadn't bothered with a key. She hadn't needed to.

The door had been unlocked all along.

When he made his way back to Samantha, he found her in bed but awake. She'd gotten rid of the towel and combed her hair, so it looked like a sleek river spilling over the sheets. She turned to him, propping herself up on one elbow as he slid in next to her. "You said that your brother was in the mansion last week. Why?" she asked, her voice thoughtful and quiet.

"I'm not certain, but I believe he still considers it home." Daniel sighed, wishing he had more answers. "It's a long story, but when David and I were kids we used to paint together . . . in the attic." She snuggled against his side, and he wrapped his arm protectively around her shoulders. "He insisted that we paint the other evening and, as nearly as I can piece together, he was bringing his canvas to the attic."

She pulled back to look at him, her face registering fatigue but her eyes lit with new interest. "There's a painting of the mansion in an antique store downtown. Did you paint it?"

He nodded. "A long time ago. A friend of mine named Leonard Moses owns that shop. He's staying with David tonight."

"I met him at the shop." An odd expression crossed her face as she said the words, and Daniel got the distinct impression something was wrong.

"Moses is the only person in Scottsdale, other than you, who knows about David." He picked up a strand of her still-damp hair, curling the auburn satin around his finger, and she laid her head back against his chest.

"He doesn't like me," she said unexpectedly.

Daniel's fingers stilled. The idea of Moses disliking anyone without an ironclad reason was laughable, but he could tell she was serious. "Why do you say that?"

"I'm not sure." She trailed her fingers over his chest.

Her words were laced with sleepiness, and the sultry tone caught him off guard. She still wore the gauzy cotton robe she'd slipped into earlier, and he couldn't help but recall the way it clung to her breasts and hips. "Moses is harmless," he whispered, but his thoughts had turned elsewhere.

Samantha's natural honesty had blazed into raw passion when they made love. She wasn't a woman who played games, and she didn't hold back when it came to making love. That, he decided, was more erotic than any well-planned seduction.

"Daniel?"

"Huh?"

"I asked you if you realize how talented you are. There's a huge market for home portraits in Atlanta. You could—"

"Whoa, slow down. I painted that when I was practically a kid. Before the accident. Painting isn't part of my life anymore." He could feel her disapproval, though he couldn't clearly see her face in the shadowy room.

"Is David as talented as you are?"

The horrifying image of the woman in David's portrait flashed in his mind. Daniel squeezed his eyes shut and willed the image away. "He's talented, but in his own way."

When she didn't comment, he rolled to his side and trapped her beneath his body, his hands on either side of her head. He leaned down and kissed the tip of her nose. "I'm sorry I didn't tell you all this to start with. I just wasn't sure how you'd react."

"Well, now you know," she answered without reservation. "I was an only child. . . ." She reached up to trace the side of his face with her fingertips. "I don't know if I can explain to you how that feels, but I've wished for a brother like you a thousand times over. Someone to be there, someone for me to care for and who could take care of me. Thank God David has you."

"Please"—Daniel leaned back and tugged on the sash of her robe until the knot loosened and the thin fabric parted—"Tell me you don't think of me like a brother."

"Oh—" She shrugged free of the robe and slid her

body against his. "I can do better than that," she whispered. "I'll show you."

"You're fired." Samantha removed a slice of pizza from the pan and bit into the cheesy triangle.

"No, I'm not." Emma slid her own slice of pizza from the pan and onto her paper plate. She cut it into six even pieces and forked two into her mouth.

A woman at a nearby table turned to stare, then pretended to examine the menu she held. Emma glared at the woman, though the oversized, laminated menu separated them.

"Things have gotten out of control." Samantha paused until Emma met her gaze. "I can't risk your safety. Not now that I've received a threat here in Scottsdale."

She had chosen her wording carefully: *a threat here in Scottsdale.* She didn't tell Emma that the message had been faxed, or that someone had entered the mansion. What was the point? It wouldn't change anything, it would only unnerve Emma as it had her.

"Okay, okay, I'm fired." Emma raised her voice, and the woman at the nearby table cast a second curious glance over her menu. Emma smiled sweetly in her direction before returning her attention to the pizza. "God, I hate this town," she muttered, her expression venomous. But when she looked up again, the hostility was gone, replaced by a look of concern. "You will let me come back when all this mess with DiCarlo is straightened out, won't you?"

"That's a promise." Samantha sighed with relief.

"Which reminds me. . . . You've also promised to get in touch with Francis today, right? He may be the resident local yokel when it comes to law enforcement, but it's better than nothing."

Samantha threw up her hands. "Deal." She was relieved that Emma had dealt with the news with her usual analytical nature, treating the threat like a mere nuisance instead of reacting with fear or anger.

"Good." Emma took a swig from the oversized glass of iced tea, then added a second slice of pizza to her now empty plate. "Stop slow-poking around with that, and let's get to the good part. Shopping."

"Good idea." Samantha had no inclination to try to match Emma's appetite, but she figured she could hold her own when it came to shopping. "Are you looking for anything in particular?"

"No." Another slice of pizza disappeared in a flash. "But I figured you could use the company, and I needed to get out of the house."

"Thanks. I do appreciate the company."

She tried not to overanalyze Emma's mood swings, but that was exactly what she'd been doing lately. Her stomach was in knots, and she moved her plate of uneaten pizza to one side. After taking a long sip of iced tea, she leaned back in her chair, trying to release the worry that swirled, uninvited, in her mind.

The strong slant of autumn sun warmed away the usual bite of the wind, making the day a perfect blend of summer and winter. She'd never been one to claim any season as her favorite. It was the changing of the seasons, instead, that she loved. The crisp fall air was tinged with the spicy scent of fallen leaves, and she found herself inhaling deeply as if to cleanse away the feeling of dread.

"You look more like you need a nap than a shopping excursion."

Samantha jumped, almost surprised to hear Emma's voice. "I'd be lying if I said that didn't sound heavenly." She stifled a yawn. "But if I sleep now, I'll just be up all night jumping at shadows. It's better if I'm exhausted when I crawl into bed."

"My husband said the fire burned until close to three in the morning."

"I didn't know he was there." She looked at Emma and found the other woman watching her intently. "I know it's not my house, but thank him for me anyway. The community really turned out last night. I don't think the fire crews could have done it without them."

Emma stood abruptly and looped her purse over her shoulder. "Are you ready?"

"Uh, yeah." Samantha added a tip to the table and grabbed her purse. "Ready."

They walked from the café toward the business district, stopping to admire the quilts and other local wares that lined the sidewalk. Samantha couldn't resist another jar of pear preserves and ended up buying a plant stand as well. She admired it as they walked. Handcrafted of rich cherry, it would be beautiful topped with a fern.

Her mind flashed to her Atlanta apartment, to the clean lines of white leather, the chrome-and-glass tables that furnished her living room. Where, exactly, would the rich wood tones of the plant stand and the old-fashioned sentiment of a fern fit in? They wouldn't. But they would be gorgeous next to the arched windows in the living room in the west wing of the mansion when it was complete.

She almost groaned out loud as she realized the path her thoughts had taken. Her mind was definitely getting ahead of logic.

"You're not going in there, are you?"

She'd paused in front of Leonard Moses's antique shop without intending to. A flash of movement caught her eye through the glass door, and she cupped her hands to see through the glare. A second flash of movement came from the back room. Since the sign on the door read Closed, the figure was most likely Leonard Moses.

"It's closed." Emma's voice was laced with a tone of distaste. Or was it merely Samantha's imagination?

She placed her hand on the smudged brass handle and pushed, feeling the door give slightly. It wasn't locked. She turned to Emma. "I think the owner is in the back, and I need to ask him about a painting I spotted the other day. Do you want to come with me?"

"No." Emma glanced at the glass storefront. "You go ahead. I'll check out that place across the street."

"Okay." Relief poured through Samantha. But why? she wondered. It was true that she'd hoped to speak with Mr. Moses alone, but it wasn't as if she planned an in-depth discussion of Daniel's secrets. "I'll only be a minute."

She hesitated, watching while Emma crossed the road, then pushed open the door to the antique shop. "Mr. Moses?" she called.

There was only silence and the faint echo of her voice.

She laid her plant stand down on the checkout counter. "Mr. Moses?"

"I'm sorry but the shop is closed." His voice came from the storage room.

Samantha paused only a moment before walking around the counter and stepping into the back room. She entered just in time to see Mr. Moses take a long sip from a silver flask. The flask disappeared into his jacket pocket the instant he noticed her.

"I'll open back up tomorrow," he said, adjusting his glasses on his nose. "Oh—it's you."

"Yes." She smiled, relieved that he recognized her. "Daniel has told me so much about you that I thought I'd drop back by and say hello."

"Oh, I see." He fidgeted with the zipper to his jacket until it was pulled midway to his chest.

The flask, she thought. But was there more to it than that? As before, she got the distinct impression that she made him nervous.

"I hope it's okay that I dropped in." She gestured toward the front door. "It was unlocked and I wanted to try and cajole you out of the painting of the Caldwell place." She smiled again and took a few steps toward him. "I also wanted to let you know my intentions—"

Leonard Moses backed up several feet, and she noticed a sheen of perspiration beaded on his forehead, despite the chill in the storage room. He glanced anxiously at the floor as she neared.

"I think it would be a tragedy if the painting didn't stay in the Caldwell family." She ran her hands over her arms, wishing she'd chosen a sweater instead of the thin cotton poet's blouse. She was trembling, though she couldn't entirely attribute it to the chill of the room. "I wanted to let you know that I intend to give the painting to Daniel. If you're willing to part with it, that is."

Realizing he wasn't listening, she followed Mr. Moses's gaze to a corner of the room. Leaning against a dusty cardboard box was a portrait that could only be of her. She instantly checked the lower right-hand corner and found Daniel's initials. Her heart leaped in her chest. He'd said that he and David had painted recently, but he had chosen her as his subject?

She knelt down on the storeroom floor, the grit piercing her knees despite the thick fabric of her blue jeans. She ran her finger along the surface of the canvas, temporarily forgetting that she wasn't alone. The paint was dry, but the slight tackiness of it told her it had been done recently.

It was incredible. She smiled. Despite the fact that he'd made her appear more glamorous than she'd ever looked in her life. Was that how Daniel envisioned her? She felt her heart swell near to bursting. Heaven help her. If she hadn't already fallen in love with the man, she wouldn't have stood a chance after seeing this.

Mr. Moses cleared his throat. "You really ought not be back here, Miss Delaney."

Even from where she knelt, she could smell the liquor on his breath. And feel the tension. What could Leonard Moses possibly have against her? There was a kindness in his eyes that didn't quite extend to her, and she felt both confused and determined. This man was Daniel's friend, and she wanted desperately to make him feel more at ease with her.

"I'm sorry." She stood and stepped away from the painting. Immediately she sensed his relief that she'd stopped admiring the portrait, but why? "Daniel and I have been seeing each other." She met his gaze and smiled. "I'm flattered beyond words that he did a portrait of me."

"That—that's good." Leonard Moses moved past her at a shuffle, stumbling slightly as he went. "Now if you'll excuse me, I need to close up." His last words were slurred.

He was drunk, she realized. An old yellow blanket was draped across the side of the cardboard box, and he tugged it over the portrait, as if she would damage it merely by looking at it. But as he turned to walk away, the blanket slid from the box and drifted to the floor.

She gasped and stumbled backward as every fear she'd managed to contain over the last few months slammed into her. Next to Daniel's portrait of her was another. And it was as frightening as anything she'd ever seen.

Like a modern Medusa, the woman's hair curled at the tips, but instead of snakes it turned into flames.

The face, where the paint was thick, had cracked, drying to an ashen shade of gray. *My God*, Samantha thought, *the woman looks as if she's on fire*. She glanced at the lower right-hand corner of the canvas. The initials *D.C.* were written in Daniel's familiar handwriting.

D.C.—Daniel Caldwell, her mind whispered.

She stared at the portrait. Black pits of nothingness were where the eyes should be. But somehow within the empty swirl of black paint there was more. There was evil.

She shook her head. *No—not Daniel. It has to be David's*. The realization sent currents of relief through her. D.C.—David Caldwell.

"David." She whispered the word out loud.

"No." Moses flung the blanket back over the paintings, the dirty yellow blocking the images. He slicked back a strand of hair that fell against his forehead and in an almost inaudible voice whispered, "David is dead."

"It's okay." Samantha gathered her courage and stepped forward, laying her hand on Moses's arm. "Daniel told me about David. I know he's alive."

Moses leveled an unflinching stare at her. "David is dead," he said without hesitation. He pulled his arm free and reached inside his jacket. The flask was pressed against his lips for a long moment before he lowered it. He wiped his mouth with the back of his hand and looked at Samantha. "Believe me."

She found herself inching toward the door, her pulse racing. As much as she hated to admit it, Leonard Moses frightened her, and his conviction where David was concerned seemed almost an obsession. She shivered.

"Sweet Lydia." He walked a few uncertain steps toward an old sofa. As he slid onto it, he laid the flask beside him. "I promised." The words barely qualified as a whisper, but Samantha was certain she understood him.

She forced herself to walk back to him, then squatted before him so that she could meet his gaze. His eyes, china-blue and clear, looked tired, unfocused by the alcohol. "I know you've kept David's secret for a long time." She smiled as he nodded. "But Daniel and I are friends, more than friends, I hope. He told me that David's alive. It's okay that I saw the painting."

"It's not okay." She watched the anger enter his face. His eyes narrowed, and a muscle in his jaw twitched with emotion. "David died thirteen years ago!" His voice echoed through the storage room. "Why don't you understand that?"

Samantha stood, startled by the outburst. She started to try to reason with him one more time, to make him understand, but hesitated. She cocked her head, listening. Only silence followed the echoing of Mr. Moses's voice. But she thought she'd heard the soft jangle of a bell. Had someone opened the shop's front door?

"Okay. It's okay, I do understand." She nodded and forced a smile as she started to leave the room. "Maybe we can talk again soon."

Mr. Moses muttered something she didn't understand as she slipped through the storage room door.

She felt herself begin to tremble as she was met with the friendly sights and smells of the outer part of the antique shop. She retrieved her plant stand from the counter with shaking hands. Good God, what had just happened in there?

When she looked up to open the front door, she jumped. Emma stood on the other side, her hand on the door handle.

Samantha pressed her hand against her heart and smiled. "You scared the life out of me," she said as she opened the door and stepped into the welcoming daylight.

"Why?" Emma looked surprised.

"I—I just didn't expect to see you standing there when I looked up."

She unnecessarily smoothed the starched cotton of her blouse, then shoved the ruffled cuffs to her elbows. Had Emma heard Moses? Samantha's mind raced back over her conversation with the man. Could Emma have heard what she'd said as well? She glanced at her friend, who was busy wiping an apple off on the bottom of her shirttail.

"Want one?" Emma held up a basket full of apples.

Samantha shook her head, suddenly reminded of *Snow White*. She threw her head back and laughed, allowing the sunlight to play against her face. *You're losing it, Samantha*, she thought as she met her friend's perplexed stare.

"What's so funny?"

"Nothing . . . everything." She wiped a tear from

the corner of her eye. "I think the lack of sleep is probably catching up to me."

Emma laughed. "Make that definitely."

She smiled, determined to shake off the ominous feeling she'd experienced in Mr. Moses's shop. He was an old man, for heaven's sake. An old man who'd held on to secrets for too long. Not to mention holding on a little too tightly to a flask of liquor.

Samantha glanced behind her and felt her blood go cold. Leonard Moses was standing on the sidewalk outside his shop, watching them walk away. She thought she saw him shake his head.

David is dead. Why can't you understand that?

For just a moment her mind considered his words. She gripped the polished cherry of the plant stand and walked a little faster. That was impossible. David had painted that horrible picture. D.C.—David Caldwell. Not Daniel.

David was alive. Had Emma not walked beside her, she would have said the words out loud. Instead she chanted the sentence over and over in her head until it blended with the cadence of her feet.

David is alive, David is alive, David is alive . . .

NINE

Dr. Rogers lowered the chart and removed his wire-framed glasses. He set them deliberately on the desk that separated him from Daniel, then broke into a wide smile. "I'm just as eager to do these tests as you are, Mr. Caldwell."

Daniel felt the tension leave his body and returned the doctor's smile. "So there's a chance?"

"That he could live a normal life?" Dr. Rogers shook his head. "Frankly, I don't know. All I'm saying at this point is that a conclusive reason for your brother's illness has never been determined." He glanced again at the chart, then tossed it aside as if dismissing it. "The term *psychosomatic* has been presented as an explanation for David's illness countless times, but without proper testing that diagnosis is worthless. I'm just glad you've finally agreed to the tests."

Seconds passed before Daniel made sense of the

doctor's words. "I don't understand." He ran his hand through his hair, fearing he was about to be told something he didn't want to hear. "We were turned down when we asked for further testing." He forced his voice to remain calm, reminding himself that Dr. Rogers was a new addition to the hospital's staff.

Dr. Rogers looked puzzled and reached again for the chart. "As you know, I took on David's case just last month." He shook his head as he scanned the chart. "I see several notations that indicate further testing was requested, but there are also a number of notations that indicate that Mrs. Caldwell canceled."

"Canceled?"

Dr. Rogers closed the file carefully. "Yes, and as his true legal guardian, she had the right to refuse—"

"My mother *refused*?" His mind and his heart were racing. There was a chance that David's illness was physical, and she hadn't been willing to pursue it? White-hot anger seared his gut, and he gripped the edge of the wooden desk as he stood. "Why?"

Daniel thought back on the times he and his mother had met with the constantly changing faces of the hospital's staff. He'd recited his concerns dozens of times, made endless requests for more testing. Always seeking answers. And his mother . . . He felt the anger boil within him. She'd sat beside him, quietly nodding, always agreeing. But in the end she'd had the final say. And the final word had been no. But why? Her grip on reality had been fragile, but she'd been sharp enough to know what she wanted . . . and what she didn't.

And she'd deceived him. Guilt bore down on him, his shoulders sagging with the burden of truth. My God, he hadn't had a clue.

"Mr. Caldwell?" Dr. Rogers motioned for him to sit back down. "I can see that you didn't know." He paused, as if choosing his words carefully. "I don't know why your mother changed her mind, but what is important now is that you've agreed to let me run further tests on your brother."

Daniel forced himself to sit back in the leather office chair. He ran his hands through his hair and waited until his emotions were back under control. "Of course. You're right."

Dr. Rogers retrieved David's chart and scribbled hastily on the bottom. "The front office will set up the initial round of tests in a couple of weeks." He stood and reached for Daniel's hand. "With any luck, we may get good news."

"Thank you." Daniel gripped the doctor's hand, feeling a stirring of hope for the first time in years. Samantha had come into his life unexpectedly and had given him hope. Maybe, just as unexpectedly, his brother would have a future.

Then a dark realization settled over him like a storm cloud. There was no real future for any of them until DiCarlo was out of the picture. Not until Samantha and David were safe.

"Is everything okay, Mr. Caldwell?"

"Uh, yes." Daniel dropped Dr. Rogers's hand. "I was just thinking ahead."

"No second thoughts then?"

He envisioned David's face, the thoughtful expression and innocent eyes. David had been robbed. First by fate, then possibly by his own mother. Was there really a way to break down the barrier that had removed him from the real world? He shook his head. "No second thoughts."

Daniel left the clinic with new determination—for David and for himself. He thought of the calm acceptance in Samantha's face as he'd told her about David. *I'll trade you one crazed organized crime boss for your brother.* The honesty in her laugh had opened his eyes to her strength and her vulnerability. She'd been afraid that night, but not of David.

He allowed himself one glance at the Atlanta skyline before sliding behind the wheel of his truck. Somewhere in this city lurked a man who was willing to do more than scare Samantha. He felt the muscles of his upper arms and shoulders tighten. No one would harm Samantha—*his* Samantha.

In a few short weeks she had tangled herself up in his world just as tightly as he was caught in hers. But he'd be damned if he would let either of them fall victim to DiCarlo.

Samantha stared at the handwriting sample before her. The exaggerated upper and lower extremities of the writing, coupled with the almost destructive indention left by the pen, revealed the subject's sexual aggressiveness. She logged it in the report. It was a perfect specimen for the manuscript.

Though she told herself not to, she pulled a stiff manila envelope out from under the report. The envelope had been taped to her apartment door when she returned from shopping. Inside was a copy of the last faxed threat, along with a note from Sheriff Smitherman stating that there was little hope of tracing the source. She'd stared at it several times already, her professional eye judging the placement and makeup of the lettering.

The lettering in the other faxed threats had been altered, the writer using block-style letters or intentionally thin-lined cursive writing. DiCarlo's idea of a game. This one, though it appeared to be altered as well, was different. She ran her hand along the length of the message. *That was a close one.* The letters were evenly spaced, each the same size. She studied the placement on the page. The message had been written almost flush with the bottom. Normally that would indicate low self-esteem. . . .

She slapped the message facedown on the kitchen table and resolved not to look at it again. What possible resolution would it bring to analyze the handwriting? It was most likely one of DiCarlo's thugs, nothing more.

She pulled the band from her ponytail and shook her hair out, only to find herself tugging it back into place a minute later. Another glance through the kitchen window at the guest cottage, but still no sign of Daniel. She stood and crossed the room to the refrigerator for a glass of milk. Another look out the window, then at her watch. It was eight o'clock and his appointment with David's doctor had been at one that afternoon. Where was he?

Grabbing her notebook and pen, she sat back down at the table. "Dammit," she whispered as the milk sloshed over the rim of the glass.

Without planning it, she ripped a clean piece of paper from the spiral-bound pad and jotted down the number 1. "Edward Mintz." She said the name out loud as she wrote. The state's prosecutor. What motive could he have for threatening her? Money? Perhaps, she thought as she took a long sip of milk, but not likely. Fear? She recalled seeing a framed photo of a smiling little girl sitting on his desk. DiCarlo could have threatened his family. A definite possibility. And Mintz was the only one who knew of her whereabouts.

Except Daniel, of course. And now Emma, she reminded herself. Sheriff Smitherman knew who she was but not why she was there. She stared at the paper. Without intending to, she had written the additional three names on the sheet of paper.

And then there was Leonard Moses.

The lights in the old house flickered and Samantha jumped. She bit her lip, annoyed at her own fragile state of mind. What was wrong with her? The night was clear but the wind was up, a prelude to the storm front the local weatherman had been predicting all day. The phone and electrical wires thumped against the side of the house.

Then a second thump, followed by the sound of a dog barking.

A slow panic began with chill bumps along her upper arms. She rubbed at them through the thin cotton sleeves of her blouse, desperately trying to ward off the ominous feeling that was stealing over her. It was ridiculous, huddling in the kitchen like a frightened mouse. Daniel was late and she was anxious, that was all. She felt the skin at the base of her skull crawl, and she stood, knocking the kitchen chair over. She forced herself to count to ten, but reaching that magic number didn't change a thing.

She was so frightened that the fear was almost tangible. Every instinct she possessed was screaming at her to get out of the house, and she had every intention of listening. She grabbed her purse from the kitchen table and started toward the door. But where was she going? She realized with a fresh surge of panic that she had nowhere to go.

"Calm down," she whispered to herself. She walked, this time slowly, to her office. When she retrieved Emma's résumé from the file folder, she found what she was looking for. She dialed the telephone number and waited. A busy signal. She punched the numbers a second time, feeling the old fear take hold. Still, a busy signal. She ran her finger down the résumé until she found Emma's address: 3750 Jefferson Avenue. She frowned. If she recalled correctly, Jefferson Avenue was only three or four blocks from the mansion, directly off Main Street.

Emma had never mentioned living so close, and she'd always driven to work, even on the prettiest of days. Samantha shoved the thought aside. What did it matter? Besides Daniel, Emma was her only friend in Scottsdale. And if she ever needed a friend, it was now.

She grabbed her car keys from her purse and headed into the night. The wind whipped her hair and adhered her cotton blouse against her chest like a bandage. She slid into the front seat of the car and slammed the door behind her. Everything went still and quiet. She watched as the wind continued to whip the branches of the trees and strip the dry leaves from their precarious hold. For an instant she wondered what she was doing, leaving the shelter and security of the house to drive into the night.

And, she thought, to the house of a friend who wasn't expecting her.

She cranked the engine despite her misgivings and put the car in drive. As she drove, she kept a close eye on the street signs, watching for Jefferson. Just as she'd recalled, it was only a few blocks away. Emma's house was easy to spot, her mailbox clearly marked with over-sized white numbers. Samantha pulled into the gravel drive and parked next to Emma's familiar blue Buick.

The house was of simple frame construction, the aqua-toned paint reminiscent of a decade or two past. She noticed an old car parked to one side of the carport, johnsongrass punctuating its demise by tangling itself between the tires. The house wasn't what she expected, she realized. Emma gave the impression of near-compulsive neatness, the work she did for Samantha always in perfect order. The house, on the other hand, needed attention.

In the distance a bolt of lightning lit the sky, providing incentive. The storm was coming, Daniel wasn't home, and she desperately needed to be near someone that night, needed the comfort and distraction that only another human being could provide. She flung open her car door and ran to the front porch.

Samantha rang the bell. Not hearing a sound, she knocked too. No response. From inside the house came the sound of a television, but there was no other sign of life. She knocked a second time and cocked her head to listen. Still nothing.

"Samantha?"

The voice came from behind her and she jumped, recognizing Emma's voice only after her heart had turned over in her chest.

"Emma." She pivoted to face the woman, her hand pressed to the base of her throat. "There you are."

"I keep startling you, don't I?" Emma smiled and waved her hand toward the carport. "I was just taking the trash out. Is everything okay?"

"Well . . ." Samantha faltered, suddenly at a loss to describe the panic she'd felt before leaving the mansion. "I was hoping I could hang out with you for a little while." She wrinkled her nose. "To be honest, Daniel's not home and I was frightened."

Emma joined her on the porch and unlocked the front door. "Of course you can, don't be silly. Come on in." She slipped the key back into the front pocket of her jeans and smoothed her hair. "Excuse the mess, though. I'm afraid you've caught me on housecleaning day."

"Don't you dare apologize." Samantha stepped

through the threshold and into a dimly lit den. Again, she had the impression she was in the wrong house. Toys and clothes were scattered over a well-worn sofa and recliner, and bits of crushed cereal littered the floor. "Are Gus and the kids not at home?"

Emma picked up a few stray articles of clothing from the sofa and recliner, motioning for Samantha to sit. "No, they're at the school's open house tonight." She smiled and rolled her eyes. "I decided to claim the dubious honor of staying behind to clean house."

Samantha chose the recliner. "I shouldn't be barging in on you like this."

"No, no, that's okay." Emma sat on the edge of the sofa and folded her hands.

Samantha's gaze was drawn to Emma's hands. They were liberally smeared with red mud.

Emma seemed to notice at the same time. "Ugh," she exclaimed. She stood abruptly and held her hands out for inspection. "Let me go wash up. Those garbage cans were terrible."

From the kitchen Samantha could hear the faucet running. "Can I fix you something?" Emma called. "A glass of wine, maybe?"

"That sounds good."

"Coming up, then."

Samantha let her head rest against the soft recliner. The house was a mess, but it was cozy. Outside the wind howled, but the small house's sturdy construction made it hardly noticeable. And that was another thing that was comforting about the house. It was *small*. She smiled at her own cowardice. Heck, if anyone was in this house, you'd know it. Especially if they stepped on a squeaky toy.

Emma handed her a glass of wine over the back of the recliner. "It's not expensive, but it has the same end result."

"Thanks." Samantha took a sip and had to concentrate on not making a face. The wine was, quite frankly, awful. She turned the stem between her thumb and forefinger and wondered what to say. "I heard a noise," she finally blurted out. "I'm afraid my bravery didn't stand up to it."

Emma folded her legs beneath her on the sofa. "Why? I mean, I know you have every right to be frightened, but has something else happened?"

Samantha took another sip of wine and wished the glass didn't contain such a generous amount. She'd been forced to tell Emma that the death threats had followed her to Scottsdale, but had managed to keep the most frightening details to herself. Tonight, though, she was tempted to confess all that had happened. She sighed and again leaned her head back against the back of the recliner. No, what she really needed was refuge from the emptiness of her apartment, a little companionship until Daniel returned. It wouldn't do either of them any good to dwell on the details.

"No. It's just that Daniel went—" Samantha cut her own sentence off. Good Lord, had she really almost blurted out that Daniel had an appointment with David's doctor? "Daniel isn't home and I felt so alone." She smiled. "Thanks for letting me come over."

"Sure. Anything I can do to help."

When Samantha opened her eyes, she caught Emma glancing at her watch. She started to ask again if she was keeping Emma from something, then hesitated. It was so comfortable and relaxing at Emma's, she hardly wanted to move a muscle. The last thing she wanted to hear was that Emma needed to be somewhere else.

"Daniel and you seem to be getting along well," Emma continued. "Do I detect a budding romance?"

Samantha drank more wine and closed her eyes again. It was rude not to answer Emma right away, but she was so tired her thoughts would hardly form. Heck, she could barely stay awake, much less talk. Finally she opened her eyes. "Daniel's the most incredible man I've ever met."

Emma nodded. "Well, I guess that just about says it all." She glanced at her watch again. "Listen, you look beat. Gus and the kids will be home in a few minutes and this place is going to be louder than an international airport. What do you say I drive you home and keep you company until you feel safe?"

"You don't mind?" Samantha was amazed at how light-headed one glass of wine had made her feel, and she wasn't about to trust herself to drive. Besides, she was feeling better already, and the idea of getting some sleep no longer sounded like an impossibility.

"Not at all." Emma stood and held her hand out for the wineglass. When Samantha started to hand it to her, she smiled. "Don't you want to finish it? Remember, I'm driving."

The wine had stopped tasting so awful several minutes ago, so Samantha drained the last of it and handed the glass to Emma. Her mind focused on Daniel, and she suddenly had the urge to be back at the apartment. Maybe he was home by now.

The five-minute drive back to the mansion barely registered in her mind, and before she knew it, Emma had pulled in front of the house. "Do you want me just to drive your car over in the morning?" She waited until Samantha met her gaze before she continued. "Now that you know how close I live."

"No, that's okay." Samantha pulled her purse into her lap and stifled a yawn. "I'll get Daniel to drive me over tomorrow if that's okay with you."

"Okay by me." She nodded toward the mansion. "It looks like you've already got company."

Samantha didn't try to hide her delight at seeing Daniel standing on the front porch. "Oh, good," she whispered.

"See?" Emma smiled at her. "Everything is going to work out just fine."

For a moment the interior light spilled out of the house, silhouetting Daniel and Samantha. The concerned look on his face and the intimate way he held her arm were disgusting. What a joke that he thought he could protect her. A cloud passed over the moon and the cover of darkness was a welcome relief. It was good that they were lovers. That way they would be too caught up in each other to notice anything else. At least until it was too late.

Daniel met her halfway up the stairs. He grabbed her upper arm, then turned to stare at Emma's car as it disappeared into the night. "Where in the hell," he muttered through clenched teeth, "have you been?"

"At Emma's." Why was he angry? Samantha wondered. She'd waited for him, had fought the shadows and the fear alone, and he was angry with her? She lifted her chin to meet his eyes and fought a wave of dizziness. "Where have you been?"

"Atlanta."

That covered a lot of ground, she thought. His appointment with David's doctor had been at one o'clock. He should have been home hours ago. But there was something in his eyes—something more than anger—that made her resist challenging him. He dropped her arm, and she climbed the porch stairs alone.

She hesitated when she reached the top step and turned to find him staring after her.

"I was worried about you." His voice was low, his eyes soft with emotion.

"You shouldn't have been. I was—"

"I shouldn't have been?" His eyes turned angry again, and he was beside her in no time. "What were you thinking leaving the apartment like that?"

"Like what?"

He grabbed her by the arm a second time and pulled her through the doorway. She felt the door slam behind her more than she heard it, and hugged her arms against her chest. An hour ago all she'd wanted was to see Daniel. Now she wanted just to sit down—to close her eyes and cover her ears and make the world go away.

"The kitchen"—Daniel's voice was hoarse with restrained emotion—"looks like it's been ransacked."

He was tugging on her arm again, and she had no choice but to follow. One foot in front of the other, she stumbled along behind him until she was standing in the kitchen doorway, seeing the room through his eyes. A puddle of milk had pooled in the center of the table and a steady drip had created a second pool on the floor. The chair was still lying on its back, several feet from the table.

Their gazes settled on the sheet of notebook paper at the same time. Daniel crossed the short distance and lifted the paper, his expression unreadable. "And what is this, Samantha? A list of suspects?"

"Yes." She watched the color drain from his face and remembered with horror that his name was listed. She shook her head, trying to gather her jumbled thoughts. "You don't understand. I heard a noise and—"

He slammed the paper onto the table with his palm. "Why is my name on that list?" He crossed the room to stand in front of her. His expression was angry, but his touch was gentle as he cradled her face between his hands, forcing her gaze to meet his. "Why, Samantha?"

"I was frightened," she whispered. "I just needed to try and make sense of it all." She pulled free of his touch and glanced toward the kitchen table. "The list was of people who knew I was here."

"Dammit." He groaned and pulled her head against his shoulder. "Never mind. I thought . . . I thought DiCarlo had you."

"I'm sorry." She felt the room spin and clutched his shoulder. "The list—I never meant . . ."

"Tell me you're not afraid of me."

"No." Tears slid down her cheek and onto Daniel's shirt. "I'm not afraid of you."

"I would never hurt you." He lifted her head from his shoulder and kissed a tear from her cheek. "I would die for you, Samantha."

Her knees felt weak, and any doubt she'd harbored melted away. "Make love to me, Daniel."

Daniel had heard those words pass her lips before, and once before he'd denied her. But not tonight. To-night he'd experienced what his life might be like without Samantha, and it had turned him inside out. He meant what he'd said. He'd die before he lost her.

"Yes."

Her eyes looked tired, and the reality of all she'd endured hit him full force. He slipped one arm beneath her knees and lifted her. She didn't argue. Instead, he felt her body relax, her head rest contentedly against his shoulder. But when he carried her to the bedroom and laid her on the mattress, her hands wrapped firmly around his neck and she pulled him to her.

She tasted of wine and desire. The alcohol surprised him, but when her mouth opened beneath his in a sweet invitation, the thought drifted away. He loved the taste of her, the feel of entering her mouth with his tongue as he'd soon enter her body. And his body was ready, his erection hard and pulsing with anticipation.

He pulled his shirt from his jeans and impatiently tugged at the buttons until he was free from it. He watched Samantha's eyes as her gaze flowed over him. Her face was lit with desire, beautiful in the half-light of the bedroom. She lifted her hand to trace the line of his shoulders, then the corner of his lips. Their eyes locked, and his gaze never left hers as he pulled the tip of her finger into his mouth.

He felt himself grow harder as passion altered her expression and her lips parted with languorous desire. She lifted her upper body from the bed and released the single button of her ruffled blouse. As she pulled it over her head, a deep auburn cascade of hair fell carelessly about her shoulders. Her lips looked swollen from his kisses, her eyes infused with need. Without a word she unhooked her bra and cast it aside, offering her body to him without hesitation.

He groaned as he pulled her against him, feeling her hardened nipples against the skin of his chest. Pulling back to look at her, he felt a certain possessiveness as his gaze fell on her breasts. From the gentle round form to the dark circle of her nipples, she was perfect. She was Samantha. His pulse raced as he pulled her to the edge of the bed. With one hand he tugged the soft denim from her hips, taking her panties with them. Her long legs draped temptingly across the white sheet, her body fully exposed.

He resisted the urge to lower his mouth to her breasts. Instead he unfastened his jeans and pushed them down, feeling the stir of new excitement as his body was freed from the binding material. They'd made love the first time in a rush, and this time he wanted to take it slowly, to memorize every inch of her body.

He started with her breasts.

First one, then the other nipple was circled with the edge of Daniel's tongue. He trailed kisses between each breast until Samantha thought she'd scream with anticipation. She felt herself grow warmer, damper, each time his mouth met the crest of her breasts. He paused and pulled her lower lip into his mouth, and she felt his erection brush between her legs, pressing lightly against her most intimate flesh.

His fingers entwined with hers and he lifted her hands above her head, never moving his mouth from hers. He entered her then, the hardened length of him seeking and finding her without guidance. She gasped as her body expanded to take in the full length of him, and he covered her lips with his. His tongue began to thrust rhythmically inside her mouth, though their bodies remained still.

When she stirred beneath him, he answered her need by moving within her . . . slowly at first, then with more urgency until the thrusts of his hips matched that of the sweet assault of his tongue.

She felt at once removed from her body and deliciously within it. Every sensation of Daniel's lovemaking pulled her more certainly toward release. When he withheld his kisses to tug one nipple into his mouth, she knew she couldn't wait any longer.

"Daniel . . ."

His tongue slid across her breasts until the other nipple slipped into his mouth. She found her release as he suckled, her hips bucking to take him as deeply inside her as possible. He pushed into her, fulfilling her need and, with a deep groan, satisfying his own.

Her body relaxed beneath Daniel's as the heady feeling of release poured through her, and she pressed a kiss against his neck. He rolled them to one side and cradled her body to his. "You amaze me," he whispered against the nape of her neck.

Samantha smiled. She wanted to respond but couldn't seem to form any words. Her legs began to tremble uncontrollably, and she felt a pang of fear. She pressed them against the mattress and willed her body to relax, to think of Daniel. He was more than her lover. Somewhere along the way, she'd given him her heart and soul. How could she possibly put that into words? She balled her fists to keep her fingers from shaking.

Daniel kissed her ear and raised up on one elbow. "Are you okay?"

She tried to smile, but the muscles of her cheek spasmed with the effort. Lord, she was tired, yet her body literally hummed with a surreal energy. Maybe it was the fear she'd suffered earlier. It had taken something from her. And the elation of Daniel coming home, the physical exertion of making love with him, had all sapped her energy. She needed to sleep.

Finally she nodded. "Just tired."

He smoothed her hair away from her neck and began to massage her shoulders, his hands moving against the taut muscles in lazy circles. She felt her body vibrating with a strange sensation, a deep trembling that started in the core of her and traveled outward to her arms and legs. She squeezed her eyes shut and hoped the feeling would pass. It didn't. Instead, it increased until her ears were ringing with the same sensation. It was surrounding her, sucking her into an odd world of her own.

She felt as if she were leaving Daniel behind.

"David is dead." Mr. Moses's words were as clear as if he'd whispered them in her ear.

Was she hallucinating? She reached out to touch Daniel's hand, to reassure herself that he was still with her.

"Are you sure you're okay?" he asked. "You're trembling."

She heard his voice and felt the shaking subside somewhat. Maybe she was just tired after all. She would sleep, then when she woke the strange feeling would be gone.

"Sweet Lydia. I promised."

Her eyes flew open. Where had those words come from? She rolled onto her back, glancing frantically about the room. The bedside light cast a soft glow over the bed, and her gaze met Daniel's worried frown.

Why *had* Mr. Moses insisted that David was dead? It didn't make sense. The vibration became louder in her ears and she rubbed them, willing away the dream-like feeling.

"I—I need to meet David." The words left her mouth in a rush and seemed as loud as if she'd screamed them.

Need. She'd said it. In her mind it sounded like an admission of guilt, a confession of the doubt that had grown in her mind all day. She needed to meet David to prove that he existed. And to prove . . . what? That the man she was in love with was telling the truth? Her thoughts were spinning out of control. She wadded the sheet in her fist and turned to face Daniel.

When she looked into his eyes, he didn't seem surprised. Maybe she hadn't shouted the words. Or perhaps she'd only thought them and hadn't actually said them. It was hard to tell with the roaring in her ears. If only it would stop . . .

This time she would be certain she said it. And this time she would say it loud enough to be heard. She forced her trembling arms to support her as she pulled herself upright and onto the pillows. She waited until the room stopped spinning, then met Daniel's gaze.

She found she couldn't entirely unclench her jaw, but in loud, even words she said, "I want to meet David. Now."

TEN

Daniel examined Samantha's face, searching for the reason she'd blurted out that she wanted to meet his brother. Twice. But he honestly couldn't tell what was going through her mind. They'd just made love to each other and all he wanted to do was hold her. But suddenly she wanted to see David.

"Okay," he answered.

She clasped her hands in her lap, twisting them back and forth. "J-just like that?"

He nodded. "Just like that. David is part of my life. If you and I are going to be together, you'll have to accept that, accept him."

Her lips parted and he thought he detected a faint smile, but she didn't say anything.

He leaned over and kissed the tip of her nose, thinking how utterly gorgeous she looked after making love. That, he decided, was how he intended to keep her looking . . . or at least as often as possible.

He watched her eyes close, then open to focus on him again. She was exhausted, body and soul. God, he loved her. He'd waited his whole life to find her. He wouldn't lose her to DiCarlo. He wouldn't lose her, period. He leaned down, his lips brushing her ear as he whispered, "I want you to stay with me, Samantha. Forever."

She shook her head, her eyes still closed. For a moment he thought he'd said the wrong thing. Then her mouth moved, soundlessly forming the words, "I love you."

He stroked her face. "I love you too."

Her hand encircled his wrist, and when her eyes opened a second time, they were filled with tears. "I saw the painting," she whispered. Her fingers trembled against his skin, her grip and her voice laced with panic.

At first her words didn't make sense, then it became all too clear. "Oh God. You saw the painting David did?"

"It—it was horrible." The words came out as a stutter, and she clasped her hand against the base of her throat.

Why had she waited until now to tell him? Was that why she'd gone to Emma's that night, she was frightened of David after all? "But how did you—"

"Shopping." She swallowed hard, and he thought her eyes looked out of focus. "Emma and I . . . went to Mr. Moses's antique shop."

Daniel felt a surge of panic. Moses was supposed to have been watching David all day while he was in Atlanta. He'd looked in on them as soon as he'd gotten home, and they'd both been sleeping.

"He'd been drinking." Samantha's grip on his wrist tightened. "I told him that I understood about the painting, that I knew about David. But he started shouting that David was dead."

"Did anyone hear?"

She shook her head. "The shop was closed." Then her eyes went round with alarm. "Wait—maybe. Maybe Emma. She was waiting for me outside the shop."

"Okay." He recognized the rising fear in her voice. She was upset. But why . . . why now? For whatever reason, he needed to calm her down. He pressed his fingers lightly under her chin and eased her head up until her gaze met his. "Did he say anything else?"

She took a deep breath, frowning. "Something about someone named Lydia. Something about a promise."

Lydia. He froze. His mother? Why was Moses talking to Samantha about his mother? It didn't make sense. He needed to talk to Moses, get some answers. He squeezed Samantha's hands and looked directly into her eyes. "Will you be okay for a little while? I need to check on Moses and David."

"David." She repeated his brother's name, a thoughtful expression on her face. For a moment he thought she was about to ask him something, but she didn't. Instead she smiled and reached out to stroke his face. "Your brother," she whispered.

He smiled at the simple quality of her words. She

was truly exhausted. "My brother," he repeated, then pulled her hand to his mouth for a kiss. "You're still trembling. Are you sure you're okay?"

She only nodded, her eyes sleepy and red rimmed. "I am now."

By the time Daniel dressed, Samantha had fallen asleep. He leaned over and kissed her cheek, then did what he had to do—he left her. The wind whipped through the trees and howled around the corner of the mansion as he stepped outside. Dark clouds passed over the moon, but the storm hadn't yet reached Scottsdale.

He approached the guest house with an odd mix of fear and anger. How could Moses have left David behind to go to the shop? And, worse, how could he have gotten drunk in the middle of the day knowing he was David's lifeline to the world? Still, apprehension tempered his anger with his oldest friend. Something was wrong. The alcohol explained Moses's confusion, but it didn't answer all his questions.

He flung open the front door. "Moses?" There was no answer.

Daniel hurried to his brother's bedroom. David was still asleep. He walked toward him and pressed his hand gently against his arm. As he watched the even rise and fall of his brother's chest, Daniel felt his pulse return to normal. Somehow he'd feared . . . he didn't know what. But something wasn't right about this night.

He allowed himself a moment to look at his brother. To really look at him. David's long body stretched across the mattress, almost comical in its relationship to the child-sized bed. His long lashes rested peacefully against his cheeks, his thick dark curls framing his face in an angelic appearance. But the paleness of his skin only made the short stubble of beard more obvious.

Daniel made a mental note to get rid of the twin-sized bed. He smiled. His brother wasn't a kid anymore.

He left David's room in search of Moses. Now that he knew his brother was safe, the anger had returned. When he reached the doorway of his own bedroom, he spotted the older man lying at an odd angle across the mattress.

"Moses!" Daniel shouted as he made his way to him. "Moses, are you okay?"

"Daniel?" Moses moaned and rolled to one side. As Daniel caught his shoulder to keep him from falling from the bed, he smelled the alcohol. It wasn't faint. It was overwhelming. Disappointment churned with fury in his gut.

"Dammit, Moses, sit up." He hauled the older man to an upright position on the bed. "What's gotten into you?"

The transformation was amazing. It always had been. Moses could be drunk out of his mind and still appear coherent when he tried. Daniel watched as his friend gathered his composure around him like a protective shield.

"Whas the—whas wrong?" His words were intelligible but slurred.

Daniel slammed his fist into the mattress and tried to control his temper. Moses needed his help, not his condemnation. But right now he was fresh out of understanding. "You've frightened Samantha half to death. What's with the talk about David being dead?"

"Well, see . . ." Moses shrugged. "I didn't know if she knew." He pressed his finger to his lips. "David is a secret."

Daniel sat down on the mattress and switched on the bedside lamp. Moses had always looked younger than his years, but tonight his skin was gray, his thinning hair askew. But more than his appearance, the childlike quality of his words made Daniel feel something he'd never felt for Moses before: pity.

He reached out and straightened the older man's rumpled dress shirt. "Yes," he answered. "David was a secret. But it's okay that Samantha knows. I told her."

"No!" Moses's eyes became wild, and he tried to scramble from the bed.

"Shh." Daniel grabbed him by the arm and pushed him back. "It's okay, Mose. It's okay that she knows."

"No, no." Moses wagged his finger in Daniel's direction as if he were scolding a child. "Sweet Lydia. No . . . I promised."

Daniel stared at his friend. He was tempted to leave the room, tempted to let Moses sleep off the booze and let his questions go unanswered. But he had the feeling that the past and the future were about to collide whether he was willing to let it happen or not.

"Mother? What about Mother, Moses?"

Moses leaned his head back against the pillow, and

for a moment Daniel thought he'd fallen asleep. Then a lone tear slipped from the corner of his eye to trail down the silver stubble that covered his cheek. "I loved her." His face contorted with pain, and his voice became raspy with rage. "She should have come to me instead. Earl Thomas was nothing but white trash."

The words echoed in Daniel's head, but they didn't make sense.

Moses fidgeted beside him, and Daniel looked up in time to see Moses bring the familiar silver flask to his lips. He grabbed it away and recapped it.

"No more booze." The words left him calmly, but inside, his gut was aching.

What did Earl Thomas have to do with his mother? Daniel had known Mr. Thomas for most of his life, but he'd never been anything more than a sad-faced man who worked at the local paper mill . . . and was Emma Weathers's father. As far as he could recall, his mother had never so much as said hello to the man.

He knew he had to ask the next question but wasn't sure he wanted to hear the answer. "What about Earl Thomas and my mother?"

"He wasn't good enough for her. Neither was your father." Moses made a low guttural sound and covered his face with his hands. "Lydia, sweet Lydia . . ." He rocked back and forth. "How could you have had his child?"

Daniel felt as if he'd been physically attacked. He stood and stared at Moses as if he were a stranger.

His hand was trembling as he grasped the older

man's arm. "Who?" He ground the words out through clenched teeth. "Who is Earl Thomas's child?"

"I woulda been your daddy." Moses's eyes were rheumy with moisture. "If only I could have." He clutched at Daniel's sleeve. "I would even have been David's daddy. Even though your mama—"

Daniel closed his eyes. Earl Thomas had died several years back, and Daniel could barely envision the man's face. Then the image of Emma popped into his head. Emma as a child, Emma as an adult. She'd always had those dark brown curls, the same as her father's. The same as David's.

"David," he whispered. He turned to Moses. He knew the answer, of course, but he wanted—needed— to hear the words. "Moses, was Earl Thomas David's father?"

"Yes." Moses covered his face again with his hands and began to sob. "I'm sorry, Lydia. Sometimes I get so confused."

Daniel's mind was spinning. Earl Thomas—a man he'd barely known—was David's real father. Good God, his mother must have been horrified when Daniel started seeing Emma. She hadn't approved, of course, but he'd always thought it was because his mother hadn't approved of Emma socially. He almost laughed. Little had he known that his mother's own social circles weren't that closed after all.

An image of Emma flashed in his mind again. Smiling, carefree as she offered him her love . . . and her body. He'd gone away for his freshman year at college and had felt displaced and uprooted. She'd been waiting for him when summer break finally came. He'd fallen completely and utterly in love with her that summer. So in love that he hadn't considered anything else. Including David. Like an old dusty puzzle, the pieces began to twist and fit in his mind. Emma begging him to sneak away and meet her that night . . .

The night of the fire.

He rubbed his temples, willing the unsettling feeling to take form. To give him answers. He balled his fists and forced the emotions that threatened to distract him to help him instead. He'd been disappointed that Emma didn't show up that night. Then there had been only horror when he returned home. His life—his world—had gone up in flames while he waited for her.

And then she'd turned her back on him. But by then it hadn't mattered. By then everything had changed. He'd become the outcast. An old anger churned within him. He'd let himself become the outcast.

"The mother lived." Daniel recalled Emma's harsh words as she'd taken Samantha into the west wing. *"But the boy wasn't right to start with."* The satisfied tone to her voice echoed in his memory.

Then he realized what he should have known all along. Emma had known about David . . . had known he was her brother.

She'd lived in near poverty while her half brother had everything, at least in her eyes, that money and the Caldwell name could offer. It hadn't mattered to her that David was never part of society, that he wasn't as fortunate as she was in that way. He doubted logic had played much part in what she felt toward David.

Maybe in the back of his mind Daniel had known that Emma was more attracted to the Caldwell name than to him. And maybe he hadn't cared. But there was no way he could have known she would use him to get to his brother—their brother.

Now it all made perfect sense. Thirteen years ago Emma Thomas had been forced to face the fact that she had an illegitimate brother.

And thirteen years ago she thought she'd killed him.

Raw panic hit him. What had Samantha said? Emma had been at the antique shop that day. He glanced at Moses, remembering what Samantha had said about his ranting. Could Emma have overheard him? Worse, could she have overheard Samantha? If so, she knew that David was alive. And that Samantha knew.

He envisioned Gus Weathers, the miserable look on his face, the conspicuously low stock on the hard-ware store's shelves. He'd long ago suspected that Gus and Emma had fallen on hard financial times. And if so, Emma's envy would have only grown over the years. Not to mention her fear.

If David was alive, so was her secret.

Daniel pulled Moses to him in an embrace. "Listen to me." He was surprised to hear the quiet rage in his own voice. "You were the closest thing to a father that David and I ever had. I need you now more than ever. Do you hear me?"

Moses nodded, a spark of hope emerging from the embarrassment.

Daniel grasped the older man's shoulders. "I need you to watch David." He hauled Moses to his feet, dragged him to David's room, and pushed him to a straight-backed chair. "Stay awake and don't let him out of your sight." He lowered his voice to a whisper. "I'm counting on you."

Moses nodded, and his eyes shone with the healing light of a lost soul forgiven. "Where—where are you going?"

Daniel forced himself to remain calm. "To put an end to this insanity. Something I should have done a long time ago."

The kerosene fumes were overwhelming, even with the metal lid capped as tightly as it would turn. But that was okay. The drive was short and the windows were down. When it was over, the old fuel can would join the other one at the bottom of the rock quarry. It was time to replace this one, anyway. Hell, it was thirteen years old.

Samantha tugged the sheet to her chin and twisted the material in her fist. The woods were on fire. No, that couldn't be. She was only dreaming. But reality mixed with the confusion of the dream until she couldn't separate the two. She felt herself sinking back into the haze of sleep.

Daniel held out his hand, urging her to jump the ravine. She reached for him and leaped, but this time she felt herself falling. Her ankle was caught on something, something that tugged her back, making her fall into the burning pit. A silent scream expanded in her chest until she felt she would explode.

She wanted to go to Daniel. She wanted to wake up. She twisted, trying desperately to free herself. As she looked down at her feet, she saw it.

A soot-covered hand held her ankle, and a manic laugh filled her ears.

"No!" Samantha jerked upright in the bed, pressing her hands over her ears. Her heart drummed in her chest, and the sheets were damp with perspiration. She sat that way, staring into the shadows of her bedroom, until her pulse began to return to normal.

It was a dream, her mind consoled. Only a dream.

But something was wrong. Her head pulsed with pain, and her thoughts wouldn't fully form. If not for the terror of the nightmare, she'd welcome the oblivion of sleep. She tried to move her legs, but the muscles contracted painfully at the attempt. Finally she forced them over the edge of the bed and stood, waiting until the cramping subsided.

She found her robe at the foot of the bed and tugged it on. Her fingers ached as she tied the sash. She felt a million years old. What was wrong with her? She recalled feeling dizzy, as if she'd had more than a single glass of wine. But why the debilitating fatigue? Her muscles felt as if they were stretched to the point of snapping.

"Daniel?" Her voice echoed in the quiet of the house. No, he'd left. She remembered him kissing her good-bye. But where had he gone? Her temples pounded, and she pressed her fingertips against her aching skull. For the life of her, she couldn't remember.

But she did remember that he'd said he loved her. She smiled despite the nauseating pain in her head and forced her feet to cooperate. Slowly she made her way down the hallway and to the kitchen. She needed a glass of iced tea or a soda . . . anything cool, she decided, to help clear her mind.

By the time she reached the kitchen, her legs were aching and tight with the effort it took merely to walk. She leaned against the kitchen table, absently noticing the crumpled notebook paper, the dried splash of milk, as she waited for the pain to subside. After a moment, she trusted her legs with the full weight of her body. But then something else made her hesitate.

She stared at the puddle of milk. There was something odd about it. The pool of milk had become sticky as it evaporated, but a dry powder could be seen in the center of it. She rubbed her finger across the surface and examined the powderlike susbstance that clung to it. Small but distinct crystals shone in the light.

Samantha stood in that position for what seemed like an eternity. Something had been added to the milk, and she was willing to bet that she knew what it was. Adrenaline pumped through her, giving new life to her stiff arms and legs. She made her way to the bathroom and jerked open the medicine cabinet. The vial of sedatives was still there, but only half the pills remained.

Panic. It jolted through her like an electric current. She forced herself to breathe, to reason out what was happening. The milk. She concentrated, envisioning how much had remained in the half gallon. It had been almost full. Logic began to seep through the panic. The sedatives were mild, and only half the bottle had been used. Slowly, relief replaced the panic. The dosage had probably only been doubled. And she was living, breathing proof that she hadn't consumed enough to kill her.

But someone wanted her out of the way that night. Why?

She had to find Daniel. She stumbled back through the bathroom door and down the hallway. Where had he said he was going? *Think, Samantha. Think.*

Moses and David—he'd gone to check on them. Her eyes flew open and she rushed to the kitchen window. At first everything seemed okay, then she noticed it—a gentle golden glow emanating from the foundation of the guest house. The old cottage was built on a crawl space, she realized.

And it was on fire.

In the mere seconds it took for her to comprehend what was happening, the golden glow turned red and angry. Had the brush fire reignited, sweeping beneath the house? There was no time to stop and consider the cause, or for dressing, for shoes, for anything. The guest house was old, the heart-of-pine framework would burst into flames like an unlit match.

Samantha ran to the door, her legs carrying her with an unexpected strength that she could only be thankful for. By the time she reached the courtyard, the flames were lapping at the sides of the house.

"Daniel!" As she screamed she felt the air rush from her lungs. Bright lights danced in front of her eyes, and her fingertips curled into the soft dirt. She rolled to her back and sent up a prayer of thanks to find she was alone. She'd fallen, but only because her own legs had failed her.

She pulled herself up and ran the rest of the way to the guest house. Even the wood of the front stairs, still untouched by the flames, felt warm to her bare feet as she scrambled up them. She threw open the front door. The interior of the house was not yet on fire, but smoke was pouring through the floor vents and sifting through the walls, finding otherwise unseen cracks.

Adrenaline and pain pounded in her head. "Daniel!" she screamed. "Are you in here?"

There was no response.

As she headed toward the hallway, she felt her toe catch against something soft on the living room floor. Someone's hand. She dropped to her knees and found Leonard Moses lying there on his side. A quick glance at the front door made her heart sink. It was at least fifteen feet away, and he was no small man. She willed herself not to panic and grabbed him beneath his arms.

It was as if she were walking through water, or living in a slow-motion nightmare. But the hardwood floor was her saving grace. Moses's body slid against the slick surface until she was able to drag him onto the porch and into the fresh air. He stirred for the first time, taking in huge gulps of air and coughing.

Relief poured through her. "Mr. Moses!" She shook his shoulders. "Where is Daniel?" The last words left her in a terrified shriek.

"Daniel . . ." The older man writhed against the porch as a fit of coughing stole his words. "Gone." He pointed to the house as the coughing began again.

Samantha felt paralyzed with fear. Gone? Did he mean that Daniel had left the house, or was he trying to tell her that something had happened to him?

A hand wrapped around her ankle, and her nightmare flashed in her head like a prophecy fulfilled. Moses's body was doubled over with the effort of coughing, but one hand held her ankle and the other pointed frantically to the house. "D-David . . ."

She could see her own terror reflected in his blue eyes. She'd been so frantic to find Daniel that she'd all but forgotten—

"David's still in the house?"

By the time Moses managed to communicate a nod, Samantha was standing in the open doorway. Behind her she could hear Moses gasping for breath, but she couldn't go back to help. The past was about to repeat itself, and she couldn't let that happen. She had to find David.

When she'd first entered the house, she could see the smoke pouring in. Now the interior was enveloped in a heavy white blanket. She could hear wood crackling as the fire grew, the sound traveling through the smoke with surreal clarity.

Something made her glance to the left, toward the single window in the living room just a few feet away. The smoke was thicker now, and the old glass panes of the window were naturally warped, but the face was unmistakable. Looking through the window was Emma.

Samantha started to call to her, but the image vanished in a fresh cloud of white smoke. She rushed to the window and peered through the glass. Staring back at her was Emma, a satisfied smile on her face.

"Emma!" Even as Samantha shouted the word, she knew there would be no answer.

Emma's smile turned to laughter, and her haunting image was made even more repulsive, distorted as it was by the old panes of glass.

Emma.

A crushing sadness met rage as the realization hit her. Emma was responsible for this. But why? A rush of hot air filled her lungs and forced her to drop to her knees. She coughed until she thought she'd collapse from the futile effort of ridding her lungs of the smoke. Emma was no longer on her mind. Only survival . . . and David.

"David!" She was searching for someone most people would deny even existed. "Oh God." A half laugh, half sob escaped her, and the hysterical edge to her voice was eerie as it traveled through the smoke without echoing.

But David was alive. He was there, and it was up to her to find him before it was too late.

She began crawling down the hall, her hands and

knees stinging as the floor heated beneath her. Just as she reached what appeared to be a grandfather clock, she heard it. A loud popping followed by a heavy roar. She recoiled as the floor beneath her hands became too hot to touch, years of varnish liquefying and sticking to her palms as it bubbled up. Just then the base of the grandfather clock crashed through the floor, and its heavy top toppled in her direction.

Someone was there in the split second before the blackness. She was certain of it. After all, she'd seen him before—a dark shape with a hooded jacket.

David.

And then there was nothing.

ELEVEN

Daniel slid back into the cab of the truck and slammed the door behind him. He stared at Emma Weathers's house. He'd pounded on the door for what seemed like an eternity, had checked every window and door for any sign of life. In the end, he'd been forced to accept that she wasn't there. And now, with no outlet, his anger seethed, the questions grinding in his head demanding answers that he didn't have.

"Dammit!" He hit the steering wheel with his fist. The word was absorbed by the worn interior of the cab, as if refusing to acknowledge his fury. He turned the key, the powerful old engine roaring to life, and in seconds squealed out of the drive and pointed the truck toward home.

Daniel hit the brakes as soon as he rounded the corner onto Main Street. A deep red glow punched a hole in the night sky, hovering ominously over the line of trees up ahead.

No, it couldn't be. His hands gripped the steering wheel as an old, all too familiar fear twisted in his chest.

He accelerated again, pushing the old pickup as fast as he dared. Once was enough. It couldn't happen again. He wouldn't let it. He turned into the gravel drive—and could no longer deny it. His grip loosened on the steering wheel, and his world crashed down around him.

He was too late. Again. The guest house was fully engulfed in flames.

"No." The single word left him as a whisper. Daniel ignored the curve in the driveway and drove straight into the courtyard, the pickup finally sliding to a stop in the grass. He slammed the gearshift into place and jumped out.

"No!" This time the word was a scream, tearing into the night and echoing beyond the roar of the fire.

For a moment he could still see the framework of the house, a last glimpse of what had been. Then, with a final groan, the burning wood collapsed onto the foundation. And just as it had been before, there was no one else. Only him in the dark of the night, watching his world go up in flames.

David. Moses.

His knees buckled and he sank to the ground. He wouldn't survive it this time. He didn't want to. The old grief returned, sucking him into its chasm of pain. He accepted the tragedy with sickening certainty. What used to be would never be again.

Then from behind him he heard the front door of the mansion slam. "Samantha," he whispered. Hope soared within him, his body humming to life with the realization.

He still had Samantha.

He scrambled to his feet and began running in the direction of the house. When he reached the porch he saw the front door drifting with the pull of the wind, slamming repeatedly against the frame. Somehow he'd thought she'd be there. Why— Daniel didn't allow the thought to form. He climbed the stairs and entered the house.

He was afraid to call her name. Afraid she wouldn't answer. If she wasn't there, then— He shook his head. No. No more thoughts.

He walked through the living room and into the kitchen. She wasn't there. He checked the bathroom. The bedroom. His breath caught in his throat and he ran his hand across his face, surprised to find it wet with tears. Where was she? One last room waited, one last chance.

When he entered the empty office, he felt the life finish draining from him. She was gone.

DiCarlo? Ironically there was almost some hope in that thought. But in his mind's eye he pictured her seeing the fire, running toward the guest house . . . leaving the door to the mansion open behind her.

Reality hit him and he staggered outside, his arms and legs heavy, his mind turning over each sickening possibility. Dear God, would Samantha have actually gone into the house? He caught the door and pulled it closed despite the resistance from the wind. As the latch clicked into place, his last reason for living vanished. Of course she would have gone into the guest house. For Moses and David . . . and for him.

The night air was cold against his face, but he welcomed the sting. He headed toward the burning heap of rubble. For what he didn't know. Answers? Some fragment of hope that had yet to be extinguished? The wind whipped through the night, and for a moment he thought he heard voices. He cocked his head, listening. Nothing came to him but the popping of the fire and the swirling wind. Then he saw it . . . or did he? A faint glimpse of white beneath the canopy of trees at the edge of the courtyard, the same shadows that had carried the voices.

The wind gusted, spraying fragments of burning ash and sparks. He walked through it, his eyes never leaving the patch of unnatural white that tried to elude him in the shadows. He felt the cinders pierce his skin as they burned through his jeans and landed like stinging insects on his face. He didn't care. He just walked. Step by step. Nearer and nearer. He was afraid to run. That would mean he believed. But he couldn't turn away. That would mean he'd lost everything.

Again.

Something moved in the shadows, and Daniel stopped dead in his tracks.

"I have them." The voice that called from the darkness was calm, the words even and measured.

The voice was David's.

Daniel broke into a run. The shadows embraced him as he entered, his vision adjusting from the blinding glow of the fire to the dark of the night. Before him was David, sitting cross-legged on the grass, cradling Samantha's head in his lap.

It was the most beautiful sight he'd ever seen.

Daniel dropped to his knees and pressed his palm against Samantha's cheek. She lay completely limp, her head propped against David's knee. A deep gash in her forehead oozed a steady stream of blood. But she was alive.

"Thank God."

And David. Daniel looked up into his brother's soot-streaked face. David looked calmly back at him, an easy smile lifting the seriousness of the moment. Daniel understood without the need for words. His brother hadn't merely survived—he was okay. The fire hadn't taken him, and neither would the memories.

He pulled off the cotton henley shirt he wore, folded it, and pressed the soft fabric against the wound on Samantha's forehead.

"Samantha? It's Daniel." She was unconscious, but the rise and fall of her chest beneath the thin white robe was steady.

He leaned down and kissed her cheek. Even through the soot and clinging smoke, he caught the scent of her. The familiar smell of her skin played against his face, waking the hope, giving him life again. My God, he loved this woman. He stroked the side of her face, willing sweet reality to replace the fear. He hadn't lost her. Samantha was alive. She was warmth and life beneath his fingers. Alive.

Daniel met David's gaze in the near darkness, afraid to ask the next question. "What about Moses?"

David gestured to his left. Moses lay, unmoving, several yards away in the shadows.

He eased David's hand to the makeshift bandage. "Hold it tight," he instructed. "I'll be back."

By the time he reached the older man's side, he knew that Moses was still alive, but his raspy breathing did nothing to soothe Daniel's fear. Just as he laid his hand on Moses's arm, the older man began coughing.

"Moses," he said loudly. "Moses, it's Daniel. Everything's going to be okay."

Moses coughed again, and the sound was deep and thick with the effects of the smoke. But he was alive. And if Daniel had anything to do with it, they were all going to be okay. Fate had spared him the three people he loved the most. Now it was up to him to take care of them.

"There was a fire," he explained. Moses appeared to hear him, though he kept his eyes closed. "You and David are going to be okay, but Samantha is hurt. I need to go to her now and leave you for a minute. Do you understand?"

Moses nodded in response.

Daniel was back at Samantha's side in an instant. She lay perfectly still, her breathing shallow. He pressed his palm against her neck and was surprised to find her skin icy cold.

"You're going to be all right." He forced his voice to sound commanding, needing her to rouse from unconsciousness, needing to know that she truly was okay. "Samantha—please—it's Daniel. Do you hear me?"

Finally she stirred, a frown marring the serenity of her face. She tried to speak and to sit up, but he gently pressed her shoulders back against David's lap.

"You're okay." He pulled her hands to his mouth and kissed each knuckle. "Understand? You're going to be fine." Her hands were freezing and goose bumps danced on the exposed flesh of her arms and legs. "She's cold," he whispered.

As if on command, David struggled to free himself of his ever-present backpack, then pulled off the hooded jacket he wore, laying it over Samantha's chest.

Daniel looked at his brother, noticing for the first time that the long curls that usually framed his face were singed away. Was that what suddenly made him look so mature? Just then sirens wailed in the distance, the most welcome sound he'd ever heard.

"Thank God," he whispered. He turned toward his brother. "How did Samantha get out of the house?" Daniel noticed the charred sleeves of David's jacket that was draped over Samantha. "Did you carry her out?"

David's nod was almost undetectable. "The clock."

"The clock?" At first he was puzzled, then it suddenly made sense. "The grandfather clock hit her?"

David nodded again.

The cut wasn't that deep, he reasoned. The clock must have just grazed her. Another reason to be thankful. He scanned his brother for injury but found only a capable man instead.

He smiled, swallowing down tears of pride. "Are you okay? Are you hurt at all?"

"No."

Daniel almost laughed. For once he was thankful for his brother's one-word answers. He pressed his hand against David's arm and looked into his eyes. "I need to get help. Stay here. Okay?"

David nodded, then grabbed his arm as he started to rise. "I didn't make the fire." The words left him slowly but with more determination than Daniel had ever heard.

"I know you didn't. Not then and not now."

As he watched relief register on his brother's face, the image of David's painting flashed in his head. The portrait of the woman—her eyes devoid of emotion, the hair curled and flaming on the ends. It wasn't supposed to have been Samantha. He realized, then, that David had known all along. He'd known for thirteen years that the person responsible for the fire was Emma, he just hadn't known how to communicate it.

The sound of sirens filled the night, closer now, red and blue lights flashing as rescue vehicles pulled into the driveway. Daniel looked at the growing number of vehicles. In just a few minutes the town of Scottsdale would be reintroduced to David Caldwell. Like it or not.

"Over here!" He gave Samantha's hand one last squeeze, then stood and began waving his arms.

When he turned back, David had disappeared, Samantha's head now resting on his backpack. Daniel smiled, knowing David was there in the shadows, as he'd always been. He'd asked more of David that night than was possible. But he knew David would be there if he was needed. Just as he'd been there earlier.

"Step back, Daniel," a burly emergency tech ordered.

"Please, you'll have to step out of the way, Mr. Caldwell," a female ambulance driver reiterated, adding a gentle shove. Before he knew it, he was outside the circle of emergency workers, watching helplessly.

Within minutes the paramedics had strapped an oxygen mask over Samantha's face and placed a compress bandage over the cut on her forehead. Beside them, a second group of paramedics was loading Moses onto a stretcher.

"Daniel . . ." Moses stretched his hand in Daniel's direction. "I'm sorry, son."

Daniel jogged beside the stretcher as the emergency workers carried Moses toward the waiting ambulance. "It's okay, Moses." Their gazes met briefly before the gurney was collapsed and pushed into the waiting vehicle. Daniel leaned in before the doors closed. "I'll catch up with you soon."

A loud shriek sounded behind him, and Daniel turned to see Francis struggling to place handcuffs on Emma's wrists. She fought against the heavyset sheriff, her face contorted with rage, her pink sweater liberally streaked with dirt and covered in bits of crushed leaves and grass.

Daniel's anger pounded in his head with each beat of his heart. Emma. Capable of seducing him into ignorance all those years ago, capable of living in the same town without remorse, capable of befriending Samantha . . . capable of murder.

She wrestled one hand free and pointed her finger at Daniel. "I'll get you," she screamed. "I'll take all you Caldwells down one by one if I have to." She paused as if to form some new maniacal plan. Her breathing was labored, her disheveled curls hanging in her face. "It's not gonna end like this!"

Her last words were more of a shriek than a sentence, and Daniel turned away. There was nothing more he wanted to say to her.

"Why would you want him to *live*, for God's sake?"

Emma's words caught up to him and he stopped. She laughed then, the sound rising over the remnants of the fire, demanding to be heard over the low murmur of the rescue workers' voices.

Something in him snapped. He'd managed to survive the first time, but he'd come too damned close to losing everything again. He walked with slow, measured steps toward her, working to control the fury that seethed within him. He stopped just short of reaching for her.

She tossed her hair from her face, and he could see the insanity in her eyes. Not insanity born of illness but of hatred and greed. "You act like he's something special." She hissed the words at him. "They all did. He's special all right. A special little freak—"

Daniel grabbed her by the shoulders. "Shut your mouth." He glanced toward the trees. Had David heard? The thought all but pushed him over the edge. "Do you understand? One more word and I'll shut your mouth for you. Permanently." His face was mere inches from hers, and he watched with satisfaction as fear replaced the hatred.

The sheriff's hand gripped his arm in a silent signal, and he released her. Francis motioned for a deputy and handed the now submissive Emma to him. "Take her to the car," he ordered.

"Daniel." Francis's hand gripped his arm a second time as Daniel turned to leave. "I owe you an apology."

Daniel cast a worried glance toward Samantha, who was still surrounded by a crew of rescue workers. But something in the sheriff's voice made him find the patience to hear him out. "For what?"

"For the past thirteen years." Francis ran a meaty hand over his face, which looked unnaturally pale in the flashing blue light of his car. "God . . . for making sure that everyone knew Emma was with me the night of the fire."

Daniel felt his gut tighten with new anger. "You're telling me you lied?"

"No." Francis shook his head. "She was with me. But not all night. For some reason it was important to her that I spread the word that we were together." He kicked at the ground, then glanced up at the night sky. "Hell, that was easy. At first I thought it was to make you jealous. I could never figure why she chose a guy like me over you."

"Francis—"

He threw up his hand to silence Daniel. "I shoulda come to you when I first suspected."

"You suspected?"

"Daniel, I've spent the last thirteen years of my life wondering about that night. Something never fit about the way Emma acted. Then I heard rumors over the years about your mother and Earl Thomas." He cleared his throat. "Anyway, the night Samantha was supposed to have hit the dog . . . well, I knew it was David."

Daniel again glanced into the shadows where he knew his brother waited. "You knew it was David all along?"

Francis nodded. "I saw him. But when he saw me he took off like a jackrabbit. I knew he wasn't hurt but I knew who he was." The sheriff hesitated. "I also knew that if I was right about Emma and what happened thirteen years ago, all hell was about to break loose."

Daniel hesitated, letting Francis's words sink in. "Well, you could say that all hell broke loose tonight." His words came out as a whisper as he looked at the chaos around him.

"As soon as I heard the dispatch come in about the fire here, I drove straight to Emma's house. Something in my gut told me I was right about her. Sure enough, she was just getting out of her car. There was an empty kerosene container in the front seat." He shook his head. "She started screaming the minute she saw me, then began running back here, back toward the fire." He extended his hand. "I don't know what else to say except that I'm sorry."

He stared at Francis and the greasy little kid with the buzz cut disappeared before his eyes. Daniel took his hand. "That's okay, Sheriff. This time I think I owe *you* one."

Surprise, then gratitude, flashed in Francis Smitherman's eyes. Daniel thought he saw him stand a little taller.

"She's waking up!" the female ambulance driver shouted.

He took off running. Enough of the past, enough of the fear. His future waited for him. Samantha waited for him. When he slid to a stop before the small crowd of rescue workers, he saw that Samantha's eyes were open. The emergency techs parted to let him through.

He dropped to his knees. "It's about time." He kissed her forehead around the cumbersome bandage.

Her dark eyes were round with surprise and fear, and her gaze fell one by one on the faces of the people crowded around her. Finally she focused on Daniel and tried to remove her oxygen mask.

"No, no, let's not do that." One of the rescue crew leaned down to brush her hand away.

She held up one finger.

"She wants to say something." Daniel turned to the paramedic. "Just for a minute?"

He nodded, and Daniel eased the mask from her mouth. "What is it, Samantha?"

She took a deep breath that ended in a cough. Finally, she caught her breath and reached up to caress his face, her love surrounding him without the need for words. A tentative smile crossed her face, her eyes questioning. "Where's David . . . ?"

Daniel glanced at the small crowd, at the local volunteer workers who were looking at one another with puzzled expressions. How could he explain?

A deep frown wrinkled her brow, and her eyes shifted back to the faces of those who surrounded her, frantically searching. "David?" She called his brother's name, the panic sifting through the raspy strains of her voice. "David!"

Daniel watched the small crowd part as his brother stepped into the circle of onlookers. Gasps of surprise and murmurs of frantic explanation echoed around them. Tears filled his vision as David walked slowly toward them, his posture timid and his eyes fixed on Samantha. He dropped to the ground and smiled, first at Daniel, then at Samantha.

Samantha reached for David, and he slipped his hand in hers. Daniel felt the tears spill across his cheeks and didn't try to stop them. He took David's free hand, then pulled Samantha's fingers to his lips for a kiss. She closed her eyes, her smile content. The circle was complete.

In one hand he held the past; in the other, the future.

EPILOGUE

Samantha pressed her fingers against the glass and absently watched the hustle and bustle of the city below. Though sunlight painted the sides of the skyscrapers in a golden glow, the wind was insistent. It whipped down the streets and alleyways, lifting the hems of coats and threatening to steal scarves and hats.

A few holiday decorations had been erected, marking the passage of time. She touched her forehead, still surprised to find the wound healed. It was almost as if it had never happened.

"It's finally over," she whispered.

Warm, strong arms wrapped around her waist. "Yes, it is." Daniel's mouth was against her neck, and the soft brush of his breath near her ear sent chill bumps scattering across her arms. "You were brave in that courtroom yesterday. You know that, don't you?"

"I was scared to death."

"Well, now Dante DiCarlo can't touch you anymore, not from his prison cell. And from what the newspapers are reporting, his house of cards is tumbling down around him. He has no power left."

She leaned into his embrace, enjoying the solitude of the moment, embracing the truth in his words. From behind them a mechanical bell sounded, paging an anonymous doctor and reminding her that they weren't alone. She turned to face Daniel, then checked her watch. "How much longer?"

"I don't know. It's been nearly—"

"Mr. and Mrs. Caldwell?"

Samantha jumped, both at the unexpected sound of the nurses' voice and at her words. Mrs. Caldwell. She smiled. She'd been Mrs. Caldwell for nearly two months, and it hadn't ceased to thrill her.

She and Daniel turned to face the young nurse. Her dark hair was pulled severely from her forehead, but that only accentuated her heart-shaped face and gray eyes. She wore no makeup, her nurse's uniform conservative. Scrubbed clean, Samantha thought, an expression her mother would have used to describe the woman's wholesome look.

Samantha nervously twisted her mother's wedding ring, which now rested next to the wedding band Daniel had chosen for her.

"Yes," she and Daniel answered the nurse simultaneously.

"They're ready for you." The nurse's clear gray eyes pooled with emotion before she blinked the tears away and gestured toward the two figures walking slowly down the long hall.

Samantha grasped Daniel's arm as they turned to face Dr. Rogers and David. The two walked side by side down the hallway, Dr. Rogers adjusting his normally long stride to match David's timid shuffle.

Recessed lighting bathed the hallway in a soft glow, concealing David's face until he reached them. His once-long hair had been cut short and styled to reflect the maturity and masculinity of his features, the strong bone structure he shared with Daniel now revealed. He reached up and carefully adjusted the dark lenses that would soon become an important part of his life, then smiled.

With that one unreserved smile the tragedy lifted and the future opened up to David Caldwell.

Samantha clasped her hand against her throat, determined to keep the tears at bay. This was a happy day, she reminded herself, not a time for tears.

David smiled at Daniel, then turned to face the wide expanse of window. He hesitated only a moment before stepping out of the shadows of the dimly lit hallway. It was as if he were suddenly drawn toward the world, and—she realized—the sunlight.

Dr. Rogers stepped between them and lowered his voice. "He has a long way to go, but this is a start."

Daniel clasped the doctor's hand in his. "I don't know how to thank you."

Dr. Rogers shook his head. "I only wish I could have done this for him sixteen years ago." He turned toward Samantha. "David's light sensitivity was brought on by a head injury. Your husband tipped us off when he told us that David had sustained a bad concussion from a bicycle accident when he was five."

Samantha felt her heart twist, thinking of all the childhood pleasures that had been stolen from David. Stolen by tragedy and ignorance. "It happened when he was only five?"

Dr. Rogers nodded. "Photophobia often goes undiagnosed in children. Or in David's case, misdiagnosed."

"All these years . . ." Daniel ran his hand across his face. "All those years lost."

"No." The harsh tone was out of character for Dr. Rogers, and Samantha and Daniel both turned to face him. "David's still a young man. Socially and intellectually he may never catch up to other men his age, but at least the filtering lenses will give him a fighting chance. He can learn to read. He can find his way in the world. Step into the sunlight, tolerate the fluorescent lights in a classroom." He pointed at Daniel. "Your determination did that, Mr. Caldwell. You did that for your brother."

"Daniel?" David's voice was low, so soft that they barely heard him.

Daniel and Samantha walked to the window where David still stared at the city below. He turned when they reached him, the yellow cast to the special lenses more obvious in the natural light. David stared first at Daniel, as if seeing his older brother for the first time, then at Samantha. He examined both their faces at length, then looked past them, a genuine smile on his face.

Daniel followed his gaze. "She's pretty, isn't she?"

David shook his head. His gaze was fixed on the young nurse as she watched from the doorway of the nurses' station.

"No. Beautiful," David answered.

Samantha leaned over to whisper in Daniel's ear. "I don't think he means me, do you?"

"Sorry." Daniel shrugged an apology. "But that's okay." He pulled her to him for a kiss that was totally inappropriate for the corridor of a public hospital. "Because you're already taken."

THE EDITORS' CORNER

Since time began, women have struggled to be respected in the workplace. No longer damsels in distress, women have soared to the tops of their professions. Strength is measured in endurance, and with our own fifteenth anniversary coming this summer, we are celebrating strong women everywhere. Yet for all that our four heroines this month have accomplished, they learn that leaning on someone else for a change doesn't necessarily mean weakness. Relish these women in power and watch how their control crumbles in the wake of these fabulous heroes.

Helen Mittermeyer concludes her latest trilogy with the long-awaited **DESTINY SMITH,** LOVE-SWEPT #886, which is set once again in beautiful Yokapa County, New York. Helen visits with familiar friends and family as she reintroduces Destiny Smith and her soon-to-be-ex–husband Brace Coolidge.

When Brace refuses to sign the divorce papers and claims he wants to help adopt the two children Destiny has taken under her wing, she has no alternative but to come to an uneasy truce with the brash executive. With threats from all quarters hovering over their lives, Destiny and Brace struggle together to create a loving family for two children who have never known love. And in this struggle, can the two lovers find their way back to each other? Helen weaves a tale of turbulent emotion and sweet sensuality that brings together a rebel and the charming rogue who will try to tempt her into yielding her heart a second time around.

LOVESWEPT newcomer Caragh O'Brien presents her second release, **NORTH STAR RISING**, LOVESWEPT #887. Though river guide Amy Larkspur feels awkward in the bridesmaid dress she's wearing for her best friend's wedding, she doesn't show it when Josh Kita spies her on the balcony like a modern-day Juliet. The handsome widower knows that Amy's the *one*, whether he's ready for her or not. But with two young daughters to take care of, finding time to spend with Amy can get pretty hectic. Nevertheless, Josh pursues his beautiful dreamer with everything he's got. Amy can barely handle dealing with Josh, but add two children into the fold and she's definitely out of her league. Caragh O'Brien tries to solve the eternal puzzle of attraction in a novel as delightfully unpredictable as its spirited heroine.

In **JADE'S GAMBLE**, LOVESWEPT #888, Patricia Olney gives us Jade O'Donnell, single mother and co-owner of the Cinnamon Girl bakery, and Trace Banyon, sexy ex-fireman. Jade has had her share of marital strife—granted, it was only for half an hour, but it was enough heartache to last a lifetime. As a firefighter, Trace couldn't stop a mother and her son from dying, and in Jade and her son, Lucas, he sees his chance to atone for his past. Desperate to keep custody of Lucas, Jade is searching for a suitable candidate to be her husband. When Trace offers to step in, Jade decides that he's her only hope. United by a marriage of convenience, Jade and Trace soon learn that living as man and wife is a bigger gamble than they thought! Patricia Olney bakes up a savory romance to be tasted only by those who can handle happy endings.

Clint McCade teaches a few lessons in **BODY LANGUAGE** to chief executive officer Cassandra Kirk in Suzanne Brockmann's LOVESWEPT #889. World-renowned cameraman McCade has decided that his real home is with his best friend and true love, Sandy. The only problem is, she's in love with someone else. But like the pal that he is, McCade offers to help her get her man. Sandy is never surprised when McCade roars into town on the back of his Harley, but this time something's different. For one thing, McCade's never picked out her clothes or offered makeup advice before. And what is with those funny looks he keeps giving her, anyway? As the two begin a charade that becomes too hot for them to handle, they discover that the warm fuzzy feelings they have aren't just of friendship, but of love. Suzanne Brockmann proves her talent once again when she shows us the true meaning of best friends forever!

Happy reading!

With warmest wishes,

Susann Brailey   *Joy Abella*

Susann Brailey   Joy Abella

Senior Editor   Administrative Editor